BRAVE

By S.CHERRY

Cover Design: By Ikeyma Wells

This Book is dedicated to every woman that wants to see herself as God see's her. And to my Nyla for being a leader and always Brave!

Contents

Allow me to introduce myself . . .

The first time I realized I was going blind I was about ten years old. I tried to see myself in my grandmother's floor-length mirror and all I could make out were disfigured images of that beautiful little girl that everyone spoke about. So I grew up in the dark and like so many I fumbled my way through life just hoping that one day I would get a clear picture of myself. And when that one day came, I decided to take a few small steps toward courage that would forever change my life.

It was an ordinary Monday morning. I had so many lackluster Mondays identical to this one. I was on my way into the office and headed toward a congested highway that was packed full of angry road ragers. It was my turn to merge onto the highway and then I heard, Beep, Beep, Beep, "Yo lady, get ya head out yah ass and move it already!"

Sheesh, was I really daydreaming so long that this handsome, jerk felt compelled to pull up next to my driver's side window and yell obscenities at me? Well, knowing me I probably got lost in some deep thought about where my life should be compared to where it is now and as usual my head was definitely up my butt. As I watched Mr. Handsome speed past me to enter the congested highway, I tried to do a double-take to make sure I didn't know him. I mean, only people that truly knew me would know that my head was always up my butt. Step right up, step right up ladies and gents come see the distracted, non-wed thirty something with her head stuck up her butt. I always feel as if I'm a circus freak and that people are judging me. Can they tell just by looking at me that I was so far from where I wanted to be? Maybe I should proudly wear my messy badge of honor and tell the perfectionists exactly where they could all go! Well, that was actually a nice thought, but I rarely said or did what I wanted because I was not brave or at least at this point I did not know it.

My name is Athena Davenport and this is my story or journey of self-discovery, or maybe it's just a series of orchestrated events that all led up to that one big moment. You know that moment in each of our lives where we are face to face with our calling, or as I like to call it our *tapping into greatness*. To tell you the truth, I have had this nagging feeling that there was more to life. I could feel it deep down in my bones and I had been ignoring it for years. I figured I'd just continue to rub BENGAY on it with the hope that the pain would go away. I had been on this planet for thirty years and lately I had the overwhelming urge to finally meet the woman that stared back at me in the mirror. I felt as if we were strangers although we occupied the same body. Oh how I wished I were more like the people that heeded their calling and jumped; no life vest, no training, but they still jumped. I felt that for these people life was like a weekend in Vegas playing Blackjack. I could imagine them betting their whole life savings on one game after learning to play on some YouTube video. It was like these people knew a secret that I was never told—*betting on yourself would eventually result in a win.*

Well that's not exactly how it happened for me; my story was long and painful; kind of like how it took the children of Israel forty years to wander in the desert before they had the faith to reach the Promised Land, except I didn't die in the wilderness leaving my promise for the next generation. ***Is there anyone out there like me trapped in their own wilderness just dying to get out?*** I noticed that people always saw me as fearless. I would go to great lengths to hide my fragile, fearful truth. I am 6' tall and maybe I remind people of strength or Superwoman. I can actually remember about five years ago I went to a friend's costume party dressed as Superwoman. I walked in all 6' tall inches of me feeling the man! Go there with me for a second and just imagine; my lips were red; my hair was perfect and my shiny armor gleamed across the room. I even managed to smile, although that darn body suit caused physical pain in places I dare not discuss. I felt so powerful that when I got home I slept in it and even contemplated wearing it to work, but decided against it because I was sure that would have resulted in a trip to the unemployment office.

I am a lover of love, my friends sometimes joke and refer to me as a future cat lady. And just as the myth says; cats have many different lives, I had many different loves, some were sour, some were sweet but there was only one I needed to become brave.

Mr. Handsome

Do you remember the handsome jerk that yelled obscenities at me for sitting at the traffic light for so long? Well, it just so happened that Mr. Handsome and I literally bumped into each other at the mall a couple of months after our first encounter. I was rushing out of Swertzmen's, which happens to be my favorite shoe store and I was running late for a function that one of the girls had RSVP'd me for. Swertzmen's was one of those shoes stores that was still family owned and Mr. Swertzmen was known for popping up and helping his special clients. I felt like I had the title of Lady or Duchess when I shopped here. The staff catered and swooned over my every selection; even though they knew I had a commoner credit card, they still told me how fabulous I looked in every shoe I tried on. I went with the nude 4" Italian leather pumps with the perfect toe cleavage; I'm a sucker for shoe compliments. And bedsides I really wanted new shoes for this event. I paid and waved good-bye to my favorite staff and ran out of the store, speeding straight toward the parking lot and I smacked right into Mr. Handsome. His coffee hit the floor; my phone landed in his coffee and, well, the rest was history. I guess you can imagine that I took this as a sign that we were meant to be together. I mean meeting him this way had to be destiny. ***Oh and I know what you're thinking—so let's just pause here and address it for a second.*** Why would any woman want to date a man that yelled obscenities at her? Well to tell you the truth, this question came up every time he screamed a new obscenity at me in our future dealings. I didn't answer that question for another agonizing two years. I guess you could say I'm a ride-it-until-the-wheels-fall-off kind of gal. ***Does this sound familiar to anyone else? Have you stayed in something far too long and knew you should have gotten out?*** My insides were screaming, warning, warning, about face, walk away, Hell run, do a 60-yard dash and get out of there. But I've learned that an unaddressed broken heart coupled with a bruised spirit and a dash of delusion will always keep a gal somewhere she knows she shouldn't be. So I stayed with Mr. Handsome aka Antonio. He blew in without warning like a character from one of those exaggerated, summer block buster twister movies. He tarnished and mutilated everything that I held dear to me, which was my heart and I never saw it coming. It wasn't until we were over that I looked back and realized that he was just like so many of us that are twisted and bruised, but he had a better poker face than I did.

Antonio was sneaky, aloof, and busier than the president of the free world. His reasons for being so shady always started with some dramatic talk that sounded something like, "You just don't get it," or "You will never understand," or "You do this every time." Oh and here's the big one ladies, "Baby I have to run out and take care of something." I always wondered what that *something* was. I can now laugh at the dramatic way he would get all worked up and pace the floor as if he had something profound to say. We were taking a trip to the Caribbean's for Valentine's Day for a friend's wedding. I felt unsettled for some reason. I tossed and turned as I tried to sleep, so I decided to get up to double-check our luggage, and I felt nauseated as I watched him slither around in the dark putting on his clothes. My heart was racing; my temples were throbbing; and I felt pain in places I didn't know I could feel pain. I tried to ignore the fact that he said he could not stay the night due to an emergency, but our flight departed at 7 am; what could be that important?

I knew it was odd that he was trying to sneak out in the middle of the night instead of waking me, but he said there was some kind of major leak at one of his rental properties and he didn't want to disturb me; oh how sweet. In his mad dash for the door, he left his business phone on my night stand. He kissed my forehead and said he'd meet me at the airport in a few hours. I sat up for the rest of the night waiting and watching that damn phone. Finally, I could no longer take the agony. It was 12 am and I felt as if his phone willed me over to it, and in one swift motion I opened Pandora's Box. As my fingers trembled, I knew all Hell would break loose if I kept going, but it was as if I were having an out-of-body experience. I could not control myself; all I could do was sit and watch this disaster. I searched through the phone. I didn't even know what I was looking for, but there were so many missed calls from a contact called *home*! I looked up the contact and the number did not match the one I knew to be his home number. In most cases it would be normal for a woman to dial her man's home number, but there was nothing normal about this moment.

I dialed the number; it rang twice and then I heard a pleasant voice on the other end of the line that did not resemble Antonio's. This voice was sweet and too high pitched. I remembered thinking *ok maybe he hasn't had his morning coffee yet and his voice sounds off.* Man, I was really grasping at straws. I needed someone to throw me a life line because I was drowning. It was not until later that I realized that him leaving the phone was God throwing me the lifeline that I was too afraid to say I wanted.

I stared at the phone as if I expected to get a visual of who was on the other end. I took a deep breath and asked for the man that I knew all along was never really mine. "Hello may I speak with Antonio," and the sweet high-pitched voice answered, "Um who's speaking?"

I could feel her worry as she breathed deep and waited for my reply. "This is uh, Athena, his girlfriend." Everything after that was a blur; there was an awkward pause that felt like forever followed by screams, and a muffled argument. I couldn't make out her words, but I did manage to recognize the other participant in the shouting match. I'd know his voice if he were buried in an avalanche, and at that time I wished he were.

"Get the phone Ant; it's your girlfriend!" This time she didn't sound so sweet. I know it was wrong, but I was hoping that he'd answer and claim me.

I wanted so desperately for him to tell her, "Yes that is my woman," but that never happened. ***How many of us are waiting for that white knight to ride in and claim us?*** I stood there in the middle of my bedroom floor with his phone still in my hand feeling nothing at all. And then the water show began. I cried tears for past lovers, future lovers and my current one.

Once I was done with the water show, the anger set in. I could feel the bitterness coursing through my veins. I was hot as I screamed and spit poison all over my room. Did I seriously have the right to be angry over something I had secretly always known*? Why do we get so upset by people who disappoint us when we already know the outcome of the story?* And of course the sensible part of me made it her business to enlighten myself on Antonio's dealings for the last two years, but I chose to shut her up. She would yell things like, "Hey do you believe this load of crap," or "Come on Athena, just let me at him."

Oh God how I wish I would have let her take control. *Why is it that we are so afraid to ask the questions?* If I would have allowed myself to ask him about the constant cancelled dinners, unexpected out-of-town business trips and quick hang-ups, I could have saved myself two years. *But you see girls, my truth was I really didn't trust myself to leave him, even if I did ask the questions. And since I'm being honest, his response was unnecessary because I already knew, and let's be honest ladies, we always know, don't we?*

The Kid

If left untreated, rejection can become down right maddening. Rejection will rob you of your thoughts until you can think of nothing else but your rejecter. Rejection suffocates your heart until it's dried up and the odor seeps through your pores and anyone within close contact gets stained by the stench. After Antonio, I desperately needed to be bathed in grace, but at that time I had no clue, so I welcomed rejection and today was not a good day. It was exactly six months away from Valentine's Day or Doom's Day as I called it. I had not spoken to Antonio since the phone call. My favorite people in the world Carmen and Meredith thought that it would be a great idea for me to take my pencil skirt out of retirement and enjoy some fresh air. Meredith always said it was a terrible idea for a woman to retire her pencil skirt unless the guy gave her a ring or at least bought her a car.

Meredith is my fancy materialistic friend; to her love is a business partnership. Meredith has a heart of gold but she doesn't like to show it. I think Meredith is like so many women that trusted the wrong men with their gold and as a result she pretends she no longer believes in love unless it comes with some bling; but I know that's a lie. Meredith says a gal should be able to walk up to a vending machine, put in her money and "Whala" out comes the perfect guy and until that day comes, love will just be another four-letter word that gets her closer to marrying rich.

And then there's Carmen. Carmen and I have always shared a bond. We are hopeless star gazers; we believe in true love; you know that story book, passionate, messy, all together lovely romance. I think it's her passionate Spanish blood that drives her to keep searching. I always laugh at the way she says it's in a Spanish woman's DNA to fight for love. Well I guess I was half Spanish because I stepped in that ring each and every time gunning for the knock out. We basically believed in taking the leash off the heart and letting it run wherever it pleased.

Meredith was busy pleading her case to get me out of my room and out of my head. She was in her last year of law school and extremely persuasive. She was going to be good at her job some day, but for now she was earning money as one of the city's top fashion bloggers under the anonymous name, Ginger Shimmer and this was how we got into all the VIP events. It was wild to see people wearing her trend choices and talking about her as if they really knew her.

"Here, I found the pencil," she said. Wow she was good; I hid that pencil skirt all the way in the back of my chest with the 90s clothes I would never wear again.

"Now take that sloppy bun out; it's probably growing a new species in there." I hadn't felt the urge to wash my hair in a while and Meredith would not be seen in public with me and my sad, smelly bun.

"Now, come on; we have to get there by 7 pm to get the seats I reserved for us on the roof top."

I snatched my skirt from her. "Meredith, give me my skirt so I can burn it; I'm over it!" Mary, as I sometimes called her, stood in front of me, hands on her hips, with her 5'7' adorable frame and grabbed me by my smelly bun so hard her expensive bracelets flew all over my bed.

Mary yelled to Carmen, "Would you help me out over here, please!"

While Mary and I were playing tug of war over my skirt, I could hear Carmen laughing from the other side of my room. Carmen was a relationship therapist; how ironic that she gave therapy about relationships but had no relationship of her own. Carmen was single and her call list was dry as the dessert. (Her own words.) Carmen was raw--no smoke or mirrors with her--and she hated makeup, but of course she did, she didn't need it. She was beautiful in that kind of natural way that made men swoon and their women slap them for swooning. A few years ago she sustained a heart wound from someone she trusted and she still hadn't recovered and until she was ready we didn't discuss him, although Mary had offered to murder him and help hide the body.

Carmen came up with this brilliant idea to start a charity where career women would donate high-end dresses to help fight depression in teenaged girls and she knew I had a few of Nana's goodies tucked away for special occasions. Carmen stepped out of the trance induced by raiding my closet for treasures; she walked over to my bed and my two childhood best friends began the task of putting me back together for what felt like the hundredth time.

I finally decided to put on the knee-length, sexy, yet sophisticated, black, pencil skirt. I think every woman should own one. This is the skirt that hugs my curves and says, "Hello boys. I came to play but only serous takers need apply." This was the, I'm-back-on-the-market skirt and I was not so happy to be back on the market.

We arrived at the Positano Coast in center city Philadelphia by 7 pm, just as Meredith suggested. The Positano Coast was the closest I had ever been to Italy, and going to Italy was definitely on my bucket list, I had a thing for history and I just had to see the Flavian Amphitheatre one day.

The Positano Coast was breath taking. The ambiance took you to ancient Italy; the walls were covered in faded sketches of the statue of David in Florence. The ceilings were surrounded with massive deeps blues of Venice beach. The sheer, white curtains that hung at the entrance were purposely left free of ties so that they caught a breeze. This place really demanded a grand entrance, or at least I liked to think so and the food would delight anyone's taste buds. I always paused before I walked in as if there were paparazzi waiting for me. The girls and I liked to sit on the roof top and get a glimpse of the hottest movers and shakers as they pulled up in their foreign cars and walked in.

It was in the middle of an August heat wave; it was that kind of sweltering heat that covered the air with attraction and made a woman feel sexy, but I really didn't feel sexy. I felt as if everyone could see my shameful heartbreak. Was I the pitiful girl at the bar that stunk up the air with insecurity and desperation? Oh, dear God could they see it? Could they smell it? I ordered a glass of Riesling as I always do because I am a creature of habit and I tried to calm my nerves. I sipped my wine and let my thoughts and this heat carry me away to Greece. Going to Greece was also on my bucket list and with a name like Athena I knew I had to visit one day. I closed my eyes and imagined that I was walking barefoot in an all white sundress on the Balos Beach in Crete. I visualized the wind blowing through my wild hair and the white sand sneaking between my toes, but then I had the strangest feeling that I was being watched and I could no longer pay attention to my daydream. I slowly opened my eyes and I saw him; his name was Maurice and he had me at *hell*o; well he didn't actually say *hello* but his eyes did. **Have you ever had a man stare at you in such a way that renders you speechless?** I felt like I was trapped in the matrix and I needed someone to unplug me. Oh my, he was perfect. Well they say the best way to get over one love is with another one. And I'm not sure why we choose to listen to those *they* people, but I did and I found myself saying, "Oh, love, here we go again."

The girls would eventually nickname Maurice *The Kid.* Maurice had the genetics of Peter Pan because he never wanted to grow up. I saw him walking toward me and my insides started screaming again *Warning! Warning! About face. Oh why did I not about face?* I felt overwhelmed with emotion and a little looney because I could have sworn I heard a small voice in the breeze. It whispered, "Just trust me, I love you." I actually slapped at my ear, but then I chalked it up to having way too many glasses of Riesling. Before I knew it, I was standing in front of Maurice giggling at his sweet nothings. I knew it was wrong, but I was hurt, and I needed something to fill me up. Maurice and I moved fast and hot from that day on the roof top and up until his departure, we were inseparable.

I was sitting at the kitchen table staring at the rusted edges of an old Hotpoint stove. I hated everything about this kitchen and this house and yet I spent so much time here. "Um hello, did you hear anything that I just said to you?" I snapped out of my daydream and looked up at this silver gray-haired fox; her name was Regina and she was Maurice's grandmother. Regina or GG as they called her was no conventional grandmother; she was sassy, witty and cursed like a sailor. And no, I wasn't listening to her and again I was daydreaming about finally starting my stage career and how amazing my life should be. For as long as I could remember, I had always wanted to be an actress on Broadway, but the closest I ever got was my high school reenactment of the 80s hit television series *FAME*.

I settled for a typical office job. And when I got the urge to put my head through my computer monitor as I often did, I hid upstairs in the sixth floor bathroom and sang show tunes. The sixth floor bathroom was normally quiet except for me and my one woman show; the acoustics were amazing. At home I secretly pranced around my house as my alter ego Miss Honey. Miss Honey is a retired world renowned Broadway diva that I made up in my head. She doesn't go anywhere without her silk head wrap, oversized designer shades and red lips. Nan my grandmother use to say there was nothing a woman couldn't accomplish with prayer, heels and red lips. Well, Nan I'd been wearing red lips and heels a lot lately and I didn't feel as if I'd accomplished much besides smearing it all over Maurice's face. Maybe the problem was I kept skipping the prayer part. Maurice thought I could not act my way out of a paper bag, but he didn't realize that I acted with him all the time. He actually said the thought of me on Broadway was hilarious.

Where should I begin with the boatload of issues Maurice and I had. Well, for starters, one day I overheard him talking on his cell and I connected the dots and realized that he was into a little bit of white collar crime and I thought I was becoming an accidental accomplice. We were like the bootlegged Bonnie and Clyde. You name it, he'd tried it. Let's see; he'd been a mogul turned real estate broker, turned night club owner; well the night club was actually an illegal speakeasy. Then there was the illegal hair salon with missing licensed stylist and the restaurant where he laundered money. He was the CEO of whatever would get him rich quick. With every new scheme I felt like I was losing pieces of myself. I desperately needed to be unplugged, but I was too afraid to say what I really wanted and I had no plan. I felt like a ship with no course or direction, sailing aimlessly toward a deserted island in the middle of nowhere. And my deserted island was Grandma GG's kitchen table listening to her rant and rave about how Maurice promised her a brand new stove.

Have any of you ever ended up at someone's kitchen table, asking yourself, how did you get there? GG's rants were interrupted by the slam of the front door, and I knew The Kid was here; I could smell his cologne before I could see him, and as usual he was on the phone with someone talking about the next business venture.

He stood over me smiling and then he said, "Hey, pudding pop."

The Kid always did have the sweetest nicknames for me. He leaned in and kissed me and I wished we could have stayed in the kiss for a little while longer and even though I knew he was full of it, he was such a good kisser and he was mine. He said we needed to talk about our next project, and by *ours* of course he meant *his*. I guess I should mention that Nan had left me a nice amount of money before she passed away. I always knew Nan had some extra cash stashed away somewhere. She would take trips to foreign countries and sponsor poor kids and buy a designer purse or pair of shoes--or two or three--and I could never figure out how she could afford it. The older I got the harder it was for me to believe her stories about finding bags of money. It turned out before Nan passed away she had come into a lump sum of money from my grandfather's royalties. Nan supported herself as a seamstress and costume designer. She fell in love with my grandfather who was a singer in the 50s; he was well on his way to the big time, but then he suddenly passed away. It was rumored in my family that a major label stole his music and his band was actually responsible for some of our beloved blues classics. Nan was tough, so eventually she fought the label until she got what she deserved. Pop and Nan met on the set of one of his gigs. She was a siren in her day and a master with a sewing machine and scissors. As a kid I would get lost in her room amid fabric, sequins and glitter. Pop died long before Nan did and she never wanted to talk about his career. All she would say was he wrote a few hits and life would have been different if the music business would not have broken his heart and taken him way too soon. Nan said I had the gift of entertainment just like pop, so she left me startup money while I auditioned for Broadway. Nan's instructions were not to tell a single soul about this money. She was the only one that believed I could actually become an actress; sometimes she believed in me more than I believed in myself. I could use one of her talks right now and of course against her wishes, I mentioned this money to Maurice. After telling him about the money that's all he wanted to talk about, but at least I had my wits when it came to the money. If I couldn't muscle up the nerve to audition, I had no right to spend it. And besides I still felt as if it belonged to Nan.

I followed him to his childhood bedroom; he walked in first and I immediately sat on the bed and started to bounce up and down. I let my mind wonder, how many women slept in this bed and why he never moved out of GG's house. I mean on paper Maurice Williams was a successful business man, but his bedroom said otherwise. For starters there was this old, scuffed wooden dresser with the missing knobs—he must have had it since he was eight when he first came to live with GG. Maurice didn't talk about his parents much, but I knew they had relationship problems. Next, there was the closet door hanging off the hinges; then, there was the child's full-sized mattress with no headboard and finally the dusty, baby blue curtains that I was sure came from the 80's. And don't even get me started on the size of this room which was fit for an elementary school boy and was inundated with sneakers that had no home.

My mind shifted from the past women and his full-sized mattress, and I watched him intently like a love-sick puppy. He paced the floor as he changed out of his designer suit and fancy shoes and into blue jeans, white tee shirt, red Phillies cap and a pair of white sneakers. He put the hat on backwards and smirked at me and started to tell me his plan. He was handsome, captivating, charming, and a charismatic ball of CRAZY. Yes, CRAZY if he thought it was a good idea to scam elderly people with no family out of the deeds to their homes. As I listened to the details, a sudden rush of panic set in and all I could do was bounce harder as he talked. I may as well let you guys in on the embarrassing details of our next adventure; apparently, he knew a friend that would hire me at a retirement home; I was to pose as a nurse and befriend these sweet, elderly people and con them out of whatever they had left in this world. His words started to mush together and I felt my heart break.

A tiny part of me actually contemplated the con and that's when I bounced so high I thought I would go through the ceiling. I had to get out of there, so I jumped up and I screamed, "That's it, I have to go, I forgot um, I forgot I have to be available for the cable guy!" I kissed him and ran off. He yelled after me, but I sped down the stairs right past GG and I never looked back. I remembered saying to myself, "Really Athena the cable guy?" Why didn't I tell him it was over and what I really thought of him? Sadly at that time that was all I could muster up, so I lied like my life depended on it. ***How many times have we made wavering attempts to get away?*** I needed a miracle before I ended up back at GG's kitchen table. I drove home in tears; my hands were shaking as I gripped the steering wheel. Sometimes we do things that make us unrecognizable even to ourselves.

I got home and walked straight to the fridge, grabbed my bottle of Riesling and downed that sucker, and then I grabbed another and downed that one, too. I got the bright idea to hide my phone from myself, this was the only way I was sure I would not contact him but first I called my job and told them I was going to take some of my vacation time. I stayed in the house for a week and I decided to become Miss Honey. I mean how could I ever face another old person again? I was sure I was going to Hell for these contemplated crimes against the elderly. Nan would have killed me if she were not already gone or maybe she was going to come back and haunt me. Miss Honey was where I was safe, where I got to live what was inside of me.

I grabbed my sheer, long, pink robe and oversized shades and I walked around the house this way for the next week talking to myself in an overly dramatic tone, extending my words like royalty and singing show tunes. Maybe I was officially losing it or maybe I was on to something. I mean after all, we should all treat ourselves like royalty, right? I now realized that most people weren't lazy; we were too afraid to become who God created us to be and without that connection to Him we would never discover those hidden gems that Nan always talked about. Some of us hide behind a mundane existence in the hope that it will get better while others lose themselves in worthless relationships or sneak off to meet their true selves in the sixth-floor bathroom.

A week later I decided to put Miss Honey away and shower, because my room started to smell like a boy's locker room, turn on my computer and find my phone. The problem was I hid it too well and I could not find it. As I listened to the computer boot up, I braced myself for my many emails from Maurice. I frantically searched my inbox, but there were no messages from him, but I did have five from my mom Teresa, my little sister Kristen and of course Carmen and Meredith. I set my sights on the subject in bold writing from Mary and I began to read:

"We know you're in there! Boy, did you dodge a bullet. Sorry. That was insensitive. Whelp! No more raising The Kid! Turn on the news or Google. Never mind. I will just say it!"

"What in the Hell are you talking about?" I yelled out loud as if she could hear me. And why did she need to be sensitive? What was going on? Ok I needed to call her. Oh no, where was my phone? I wished I had gotten a house phone. Nan always tried to tell me that cell phones were not reliable. Yup, and especially when you hide them from yourself. I began to get dizzy and I thought I might faint. I had to sit down, but then I realized I was already sitting down. Ok, I needed to lie down, so I laid on my bed and read the email holding the laptop over me. Maurice Williams, The Kid, was indicted on several counts of fraud and conspiracy. I must have re-read Mary's email fifty times. There was a federal case building against him and his entourage. Oh, gosh was I a part of the entourage? My thoughts were racing. My poor Kid—he couldn't go to prison! He wouldn't survive it. Ok, the rational part of me took control and I found myself talking to her in the mirror.

"Athena, calm down and breathe." I took a few deep breaths and felt like I sucked up all the air in my room. I didn't know if I should cry or laugh, so I did a little bit of both. I got the urge to pray but I had not prayed in so long that I forgot how to do it. Somehow I knew that Maurice getting arrested was God doing that saving-me-without-me-asking thing. I could have actually been arrested and wearing orange and it is definitely not my color. Once again my mind wandered to the many women that were out there in orange for going along with some plan from some man that she thought loved her. I pictured her as she sat in her cell staring at nothing. She's just coming around to the impact of her decision and the full awareness of what self love is, but now she's locked away and surrounded by strangers. I couldn't help but think about how I could have easily been her. I laid the computer on my chest and tried to absorb the email into my spirit so reality would sink in. I let my fingers rest on my lips and remembered our last kiss and the way I ran out of the house. I now understood that I was really running for my life. I closed my eyes and dealt with the fact that I would never see The Kid again and that it was really over.

The Cake Man

It had been a few months since The Kid's sentencing and I could not get in contact with GG because I never did find that phone and I wasn't one to back up my contacts. I guess that was God again. It was as if my phone disappeared. I should have stopped by to check on her, but I could not bring myself to visit her or I knew I would have found a way to visit *him*. I stayed away, but I did manage to get my sister Kristen to check on her and take her things she needed until Kristen forced me to stop. GG did have other children in her life to step up in Maurice's absence.

I guess the few months of alone time were doing me good, but I was bored out of my mind. I was back in my manila colored box typing my life away. My manager noticed that I was having a pattern of call outs and suggested that I take advantage of the stress leave that the company offered. He loved hearing about my soap opera romances and it gave me extra brownie points, so I didn't mind telling him. We shared a lot of our personal stories; he had a rough past that he refused to deal with so instead he got lost in meaningless sex. He was a perfectly manicured man who understood breakdowns and said I was on the verge of one, but I disagreed. A few years ago he said he had one when he tried to figure out who he really was and he still admits he isn't sure. Nan would say she knows someone that loves him and knew him before the beginning of time and I knew she meant God. Nan was always so sure of everything.

Oh the sheer joy I felt to be back in my box, crunching numbers and singing show tunes in the sixth floor bathroom (insert sarcasm). It was Tuesday and ten minutes to 5pm. 5pm was a dangerous time in this place and if you weren't careful, you could get trampled as everyone rushed past the puke green walls and into the rusty elevator to break free. I was all set to meet Kristen for happy hour and like so many others looking forward to drinking away the memory of my day.

Kristen is my younger sister by three minutes. We are identical twins and it would have been impossible to tell us apart except I was born with a tiny mole under my left eye. As we got older we wanted our own identities, so I kept my hair natural and wild and Kristen kept hers tamed and flat ironed.

Our mother Teresa spent most of our childhood working from home doing customer service work by day and cleaning banks at night until she started her own cleaning business by mistake. She always said cleaning gave her peaceful time away from people. Teresa was great at her techniques and before she knew it the clients started coming directly to her instead of going through the agency and the rest was history.

Teresa's entire being was cloaked in fear. We all knew she wanted to become so much more. My mother had a fear of dogs, fear of cats, fear of fires, fear of losing, fear of winning, fear of drowning, fear of storms and fear of her own shadow. The cleaning business was a front because she was also afraid of people and preferred to be alone. So growing up when it thundered and the lightening cracked the skies, we hid under the table as we were instructed. We never learned to swim; we never owned pets; we were extra careful not to burn the house down and her fear reigned supreme in our house. I always wondered what happened to my mother because she was nothing like Nan. Nan would only say that Mom was never right after our father died. She made ok money, so we grew up in the middle class and we enjoyed life. Teresa had passed her fear down to us like heirlooms. Don't try this; don't try that because you may get hurt. She did a lot of damage, although I knew she meant well.

I remember her sitting us down for a lecture that went something like this: "Girls don't go near white vans because someone may kidnap you and ride off." In high school I would literally run from any white van that came near me. Imagine me pausing in mid-conversation and backing away without a word, my skinny knees wobbling, doing my best impression of Flo Jo. I would run home to Teresa to tell her I almost got taken by the white van. Everyone thought I was a whack job except Carmen and Meredith. They knew my mother.

Teresa never remarried after my father died from a heart attack. He died when Kristen and I were babies, so we never had a chance to see how a man should treat a woman. Our first impressions in that regard came from a lot of trial and error and shared teenaged girls' stories. Teresa was too afraid to talk to us about boys. Teresa was a great mother, but there was no pushing us toward greatness, so we grew up with an understood sentiment of *settling*. The funny thing was that settling never worked out for us. The Universe would throw back our ideas of normalcy until we came to the realization that we were meant for so much more. Kristen arrived at her greatness before I did. As I told you earlier, my journey was a long one. One day Kristen popped up at my house all musty and sweaty. She was panting like a dog all out of breath, and she said she had been running for miles to clear her head. She said she realized that life was short and if she didn't start living, then she would prepare for dying. She had to make a choice. And today she was choosing to live. At the time I thought she was crazy. I got the creative flair and Kristen was great with numbers. She always had a love for math and a thing for finance. Yuck. She wanted to teach impoverished people about money, which again seemed nuts to me at that time because she didn't have any real money to talk about. She was in my kitchen yelling at the top of her lungs, "I will put it out there, believe it and watch it come!" Ok, well maybe she did get a little of the dramatic flair because there was definitely a whole lot of drama going on in my kitchen. A few months later she stopped dating, started reading weird self-help books written by an old dead guy named Napoleon Hill and going to church more. She started going to financial seminars and she even made us call her a finance coach and again I thought she was going off the deep end. But then before I knew it she actually started pulling it off; she began giving free classes on credit repair at the local community center. Word of Kristen's classes spread all over the city and the next thing we knew she was being interviewed on the local morning news. I still thought she was nuts to give up dating, but this new way of living was actually working for her.

Lately I could not stop thinking about the way we grew up. Kristen had taken all we had ever known and threw caution to the wind, but I wasn't about to turn into some self help guru. We met at Camino's, which was our favorite place to get margaritas and salsa. She ordered a strawberry margarita and I ordered the plain. We were so different. I hadn't seen much of her lately between her seminars and the traveling, but I missed her.

"I have big, big news." I listened to her intently as we sipped our margaritas and twirled the ends of our hair like we did when we were six years old. Apparently her dating strike had been over for some time, she said she met a real nice guy at a financial mixer. She had that wild look in her eyes that she would get right before she surprised me and did something crazy. My sister slowly raised her left hand and there it was, a 4 carat solitaire stone of love. I downed my margarita fast. I forced back my tears because I was really happy for her, and we screamed and squealed in joy. My baby sister was getting hitched. Damn.

It was a Saturday night and everyone was at my house, keeping lonely dateless Athena company.

"I bet you're just itching to go on a date." Kristen was teasing me and I didn't find it funny, so I threw a pillow at her.

"Shut up Kristen, I can handle being single." But actually I couldn't, I was months into this no dating thing that I told Kristen I would try and so far it wasn't working, and she was right. *I was itching.* And I couldn't wait until everyone left so I could check my email and scratch.

He was just a friend; there was no way I was ready for another relationship or at least that's what I told myself. Kristen kept trying to get me to go on another date with her and her fiancé Gary but after the last dinner, I refused to sit at a table sandwiched between those two while they blew kisses and ignored me. I asked her not to invite me on any more third wheelers. We were watching our favorite movie, *The Sweetest Thing.* Kristen and I were big Cameron Diaz fans. Meredith was in the kitchen pouring wine and Carmen was upstairs in my closet as usual trying to find a dress to swap for some therapist's mixer. The girls were hitting the streets to rub elbows with cutest and most eligible bachelors in the psychology field. Carmen had just finished her last certification and had officially earned a license and now she could see her own clients. I could not be more proud, but I had emails to check and I wanted her and Mary out.

Gary was in my living room staring at Kristen like steak. She was about as tall as I was but just a tad thinner, and we both had our father's high cheek bones, dark brown eyes and thick wavy hair, but Kristen got Teresa's pouty lips that drove men wild. She was oblivious to her effect on men and as for me—I knew beauty was a plus, but of course I was never bold enough to do anything about it.

Attracting a man was never an issue with me, but keeping one was a horse of a whole different color. And, ok I'll admit it I was a little jealous. Gary was spiritual which would have been a plus for Nan. He stood well over 6'2"; he was muscular and loaded; he was a stock broker for Metropolitan Property in New York City. At least Nan's prayers were answered for one of us.

Kristen was planning to move to the big apple with Gary, so they could be closer and it was perfect for her to really break into finance. At that time I did not see how God was connecting the dots for me because Gary lived near Broadway. They finally left me and thank God because I couldn't take another second of that new love, you know the kind of love where everything they say or do is a cause to canoodle.

I was alone at last, and I tip toed over to my computer after shewing Mary and Carmen out of the house. I was actually sneaking into my own room. I knew I should not go anywhere near my emails but I couldn't help it. Somewhere in between my hiatus I had met Justin aka The Cake Man. I was sitting alone at the J-spot, a cool, contemporary coffee shop that my new friend Jocelyn owned. I remember the first time I drove past. I just had to stop in and check out the scene. I walked in and was greeted by Jocelyn the curvy swanky blond with the bright blue eyes that drew everyone in her direction.

Jocelyn had the aura of the Dali Lama and the looks of Bo Derek. And after one conversation with her we became quick friends and I was hooked on her special coffee blends and conversation. Jocelyn and I would talk for hours and she taught me about the importance of aroma therapy and coloring a room. Everyone in the J-spot had that, "I'm super trendy without even trying look." I noticed that a lot of fashionable, actor types frequented this place. Jocelyn really took coffee to the next level; she was also known for her homemade cakes and pastries. I had a tough day at work, so I decided to leave early and go have a cinnamon latte. I sat in my favorite corner in the all-white comfy love seat. This place had all white décor and hydrangeas everywhere; the aroma was a mixture of Jocelyn's secret oils that instantly put you in a good mood.

A rageaholic would turn into a dandelion after one outing in this place. I had my computer with me, and I finally got the nerve to start looking for an acting coach. So there I was hair pulled back in a bun, and this time it was clean; reading glasses on and work badge still attached to my blazer. I tried to look no-nonsense so that none of the guys that had been eyeing me would approach. I meant what I said about swearing off men. I was deep into my online search; then Jocelyn came over to me with a piece of cheese cake and the biggest smile. Now you can image my confusion, because I did not order any cheese cake, but then the confusion quickly turned into excitement because I loved her vanilla bean cheese cake.

"So what am I like the customer of the day?" She giggled as she handed me the plate and then she rushed away. I wondered why she was acting so weird. I grabbed the plate of heavenly deliciousness and a small note fell to the floor. Now I was intrigued. I picked up the note and followed her.

"Who is this note from?" She giggled again and said she wasn't allowed to say who it was from. Ok this was getting strange.

I opened the note and it said, "You are absolutely beautiful; you should smile more; hope this does the trick; and call me." I searched around for my cheesecake admirer but could not place a face with the cake. I asked Jocelyn who sent it, but she was sworn to secrecy. Wow! This was exciting. Someone actually sent me cake. How did this guy know that cake was the way to my heart? I couldn't think of anything but this note for the rest of the day. I know I should have ignored his advances, but what girl could pass up calling a guy who tried to get her attention in such a thoughtful manner? I waited two whole days, and then I finally called The Cake Man. I dialed the number and my heart fluttered; he answered on the second ring, and I wondered if he was waiting for my call.

"Hello, can I talk with um," I realized he never left a name on the note so I didn't know who to ask for.

"Hi, this is Justin and you must be Miss serious coffee lady."

I smiled and introduced myself. I think I could actually hear him smile through the phone. His voice was deep and smooth. I pictured myself floating on his pronunciations; man was I high off this conversation, so I knew what I had to do. After an hour or so, I explained to Justin that I was not in the place to date. I thanked him for the cake and I quickly hung up. Boy was I proud of myself; I stood tall; puffed up my chest and looked myself in the mirror and started two-stepping and singing, "Who got the juice. I got the juice and who don't need no man? I don't need no man."

But then it happened. I was interrupted by a little beep, and then another beep and then another beep, beep. I crept over to my phone in apprehension. I knew it was Justin; my phone betrayed me as I read his silky text messages. Oh boy, I was in trouble.

"Look serious lady, I just want to be a friend. So let's just email until you're ready for more."

Damn, Damn, Damn, and there you have it ladies. In one split second I had lost all of my juice and so began a courtship via email between me and The Cake Man. I found myself getting dressed up just to email him as if we were out on a real date, and tonight I wanted to be sexy. I hoped that Carmen had returned my red strapless dress and to my surprise she had. I went downstairs and called out to the gang even though I knew that I had personally walked them out. After I was sure the coast was clear I went back up to my bedroom, slipped on my red strapless mini, let my hair down and caught a glimpse of myself in the mirror. She was shaking her head at me as I did the walk of shame toward my computer. So I ignored her as I often did, I mean who does she think she is to shame me. This was just innocent emails and chats. I opened my email and began chatting with Justin. It hadn't been that long since I had the cake at J-spot and I still felt like I was somewhat in control. The problem was I had that nagging feeling that I was not ready for this and I knew God wanted me to stay still but I didn't know how. We chatted about work, hobbies, movies and past loves. I was a white liar on the love subject; I decided that the past should be the past. I started to feel that all too familiar lost puppy syndrome kicking in. That syndrome had affected me since high school, and so far there was no cure on the market for it. I would meet a man and attach myself to him as If I were a wounded lost puppy. *How many women out there are stricken with this syndrome and what are we trying to fill that makes us get attached so fast?*

And then, finally, he said it: "Lets Skype so I can see your beautiful face."

I could remember feeling so breathless and silly, but I was prepared to accept his Skype call. Was I too overdressed? What would be the occasion if he asked about the dress? Ok, Athena, remain calm. You are in control and you can put on a dress any day you please, and if he asks, *that* will be your response.

I accepted the message and there he was: The Cake Man. I felt as if I were transported back to ancient Egypt because there was definitely a Pharaoh sitting in front of me. Dear Lord, save me! SOS! Carmen! Teresa! Nan! MAYDAY! MAYDAY! He looked coco and smooth like his voice; his teeth were perfectly straight and glistened like mother of pearl. His clean-shaven cut was so perfect I almost reached out to him. He looked tall. Mmhhhh and his eyes were two black pools of something that I wanted to swim in. MAYDAY, MAYDAY, is anyone out there? I knew all too well how this could end up even though I swore to myself to take some time.

After a few weeks of Skype sessions and against my better judgment, I agreed to meet Justin at a local soul food restaurant of his choosing. I started to feel a little guilty that I spent most of my time online with him and not looking for classes or coaching to jump start my non-existent acting career. I found it easier to get lost in Justin instead of what I knew I truly wanted.

It was Saturday night, and I avoided Carmen and Meredith like the plague. I purposely hinted around all week that I could not do a girls weekend because I wanted to practice a new monologue and catch up on some reports for work. Well, the reports part of my story was actually the truth. I was so far behind at work, but all I could think of was Justin. I was getting ready for date night. I decided to remix the red strapless dress that I wore before on our first Skype. I paired the dress with a light blue jean jacket and those nude pumps. I was all set to walk out the door and--out of nowhere--I could not breathe. Was I that nervous that I was having a spontaneous asthmatic attack?

I rushed to the bottom of my living room stairs and put my head between my legs, because I started to feel faint and I knew I was having the mother of all panic attacks. The room was spinning and I felt like I was losing my mind. So there I was at the bottom of the stairs in my perfect dress with my head between my legs feeling anything but perfect.

"Dammit, why do I feel so upside down?" *Upside down* was a term that I used when my universe felt off. Nan used to say it meant that I needed to stop whatever I was doing and pray. I think God wanted the date that night, but I was running and I had my heart set on Justin; boy was I wrong. I texted The Cake Man to tell him I would be running a little late. I sat at the bottom of the stairs doing deep breathing techniques. Every time I tried to stand, my world would spin out of control. After about an hour or so, I started to feel normal again, so I went back upstairs to the bathroom to wash and repaint my face. I carefully avoided giving myself direct eye contact in the mirror because I knew I should stay home.

"Wow, Athena what a great start to your date." Panic attacks might simply be our soul's way of telling us that it's time to try something else. These warnings are the great battle within, and either we change the route or we choose to stay on the course until we run off the road. That night, my panic attack subsided, and I was able to head out and meet Justin but I was definitely headed off the road. I pulled up in front of a small restaurant on Germantown Avenue which was a popular urban part of Philadelphia. Many Black-owned businesses did well in this part of town. I could hear the blues thumping all the way to my car, the air was thick and I was still a little rattled from the panic attack. And now this little place had me a little spooked. But then Justin stepped in front of my car with his 6'1",

240-pound frame, and instantly all was right in my world—well at least for a little while.

"Hello, Gorgeous, did I ever tell you I love that dress?"

Justin was a charmer just like Rece. He was well-dressed but not too flashy and he had that man's, man kind of walk that made me wish I had a remote control to rewind him coming and going.

"Hello Cake Man." I had gotten used to calling him this after the first time we Skyped and it kind of stuck. So this place wasn't so bad after all, but it was definitely a neighborhood spot. A lot of important musical history happened here. I'd heard stories of some of the most famous R & B artists sharing a meal or two and performing here. It was open mic night and between the crooning, my cocktail and Justin, this was the prefect night. I noticed that Justin kept shifting in his seat as he tried his best to ignore his phone buzzing and rattling all over the table. He finally excused himself and took the phone call. I really didn't think anything of it, because he had been the perfect gentleman. I sat there eating my delicious shrimp and grits as I swayed in my seat to the music. The bartender kept giving me the stink eye but I was in such a great mood that I just raised my glass and smiled at her. I had been so into the moment that I only just then noticed that Justin was taking longer than he should. I decided to walk to the ladies room.

Well, I walked into one of the most heated conversations I have ever heard in a bathroom hallway. Justin's last words were, "She's my daughter, too and if you nag me while I'm working, I won't be able to provide for her." Wait! What? Working? Daughter? I quickly ran back to the table. Justin's back was turned so he never noticed me standing behind him. I waved to the smelly faced bartender with the stink eye because I needed another round of whatever Justin had me drinking, and I tried to digest what I just heard. I didn't want to jump to any conclusions, and I did know that he worked long hours because he was trying to start his own IT Company. But I was concerned about hearing that he had a daughter which he never mentioned. I pictured her as being adorable with those deep dark eyes like her daddy and I decided this could be a good thing. I mean, I always wanted a daughter and the title of step mom was one that I was happy to own.

But the sensible part of me kicked in and she said, "Earth to Athena! Really? Step mom?" I knew that she was right. I hardly knew this guy and what was I thinking? Well at that time my mind could not handle another letdown, so step mom it was, dammit! *Have you ever rationalized something that was completely irrational just to spare yourself a little grief? Please don't tell me that I am the only woman that tried to trick her own brain.*

My thoughts were interrupted by Justin heading toward the door; he looked back and caught me staring so he hand-signaled for me to wait. His face expressed either shock or extreme gastric distress. I thought it would be best to listen. My cocktail finally came, and I sat there for a while staring at the entrance. I wondered what was going on. Finally I got sick of waiting so I got up to look, and as I reached the door I saw that a crowd had formed. What the heck was going on? A crazed mad woman was screaming in the middle of the street. She looked like she just escaped a psych ward. She was wearing an all-white pajama set; she had a messy ponytail. Her strawberry blond strands were reckless and wild, her fair skin looked splotchy probably from the heat she gave off and her green eyes were blood shot; she was seething with anger and cursing and crying.

She screamed and burst into fits of rage. This psychopath was throwing kids toys, shoes and everything that was loaded in her fancy mom van. I stood there, watching with the rest of the onlookers and some were even cheering her on. I moved a little closer to find Justin, but this woman scared me, so I was careful not to disturb her. I searched the crowd and then I caught a glimpse of Justin's victimized face, and I knew I had been hoodwinked again. I knew better than to get in the mix of The Cake Man and the Strawberry Blond, so I eased away with my hurt feelings and sprinted past the front door and the nosey bartender who smirked at me. I'll always wonder if she dimmed Justin out because there was something weird about her energy. There was no point in crying over him. I was numb.

I got in my car and released a scream the probably shook the heavens. I was in pain; my core was bruised and I didn't understand what was going on with my universe. I started the car, revved the engine and did a serious tire screeching U-turn. I wanted to make things worse, some onlookers, Justin and the strawberry blonde paused to watch me and Justin and I made eye contact. He looked terrified as I flipped him the bird and my mission was accomplished. I drove away at 90mph. I needed to get far away from that place. And just as I contemplated slowing down, the flashing lights in my rear view mirror gave me the final incentive to slow down and pull over. And then it happened as natural as breathing and I started to pray. It seemed like the officer moved in slow motion and with every footstep he took toward my car, my prayers were more fervent and desperate.

"Dear God, why don't you love me? Wait, I'm sorry. I know you love me. Why don't I love me? What's wrong with me? I know you see what's happening to me. Do you want me to be alone? Can you hear me? Please don't say you want me to be alone. Why am I having panic attacks? Please make them stop. It hurts, Amen."

I was a wild woman in need of rescue and in my heart I knew it couldn't come from a Saturday night date. I heard the tap on my window, but I took a few seconds to get myself together before I responded.

"Miss did you know how fast you were going in a residential neighborhood?" I turned to answer the question, and I saw the face of an angel. His tone was harsh but his face softened as soon as I looked up. I was a hot mess and although I said I wouldn't cry, of course I did.

My nose was red and stuffy, "No I didn't realize." I apologized and explained that I had a real bad day and I wanted to get home. He paused. I could tell he was thinking, and maybe I wouldn't get a ticket.

"Ma'am you could have killed someone, now I'm going to need your license and registration."

This was just great. I survived a date from Hell that ended in a speeding ticket. After Officer Angel Face handed me the ticket, he smiled and said, "Whoever he is, you're probably better off." I didn't know why, but his words eased my tattered heart. I drove home doing 23mph feeling drained and exhausted. What a night. I got to my front door and rested my head there for a while; then I went inside and shed my clothes right in the living room. I threw the ticket envelope on the table and out came the card that had the officer's name printed on it—Kendrick Ryan of the 32nd Precinct.

He had handwritten a note that read, "If you're ever in trouble call me."

Oh no Officer Kendrick Ryan, I think I've had enough notes to last me a life time. I tossed the card in the trash and headed straight for the shower. I purposely let the water get as hot as I could take it and for the next hour I sat in the steaming pool of mess, and I tried to figure out my next move.

Start Spreading the News

I spent all of Sunday in bed going back and forth between episodes of *Snapped* and *Lifetime* movies where the women murder their husbands and get away with it. I felt stupid for believing that Justin could actually be the person he said he was. Were any men who they claimed to be? I knew I had made some bad choices, but Justin gave me no warning that he was a creep or maybe he did and I missed the memo. Men should be required by law to carry creep cards before tricking innocent women into dates. I would need to diet after consuming large amounts of ice cream and fried chicken, but I didn't care; I was in the mood to feel sorry for myself. After the terrible Saturday night, I thought it would be a good idea to be serious and think of myself as a single girl. I tossed and turned all night. I could not get the image of Justin's wife out of my mind. She looked so hurt and I felt guilty.

Before I knew it, I was hitting the snooze button and it was already Monday morning. I woke up in a New York state of mind, so I dialed Kristen in the hopes that she would be okay with me invading her new place for a while. I needed to put things into perspective and get inspired. It wasn't surprising when Kristen agreed to give me shelter for the next week or two or three.

"Of course you can come and stay. You can help me with some things for the wedding, and you can tell me all about what you've been doing with your new single life." I felt a little guilty because there was nothing new going on and I had been up to my old tricks that never seemed to work out. I promised to fill her in on all of my exaggerated fabulous dinners for one. I hung up with Kristen and got ready for some fresh air, and that's when it hit me. I needed to call my job.

I felt like a little mouse as I dialed my manager's number and explained that I needed to resign. I was listening to him give me every reason why I should stay and at the same time, I could hear my own voice in my head. "Well, well! Look who finally grew a pair," Ok, well not exactly. I took him up on his idea to take a leave of absence. He advised me that he was forcing me to take the stress time because he didn't want to lose me. And thank God, I was actually terrified of leaving the place that I loathed for the past couple of years. Who did I think I was to go out and trust myself to accomplish my own dreams? I mean who would be crazy enough to do that? Well, obviously someone was crazy enough to do it; we see proof all around us. Everything we use on a daily basis, from products to services are direct results of someone's insane idea to live out a dream.

Are there any nut jobs out there crazy enough to just go for it? Well I didn't know if I was tough enough to be a part of the crazy club, but one thing I did know is that I was tired of rubbing Bengay on my broken dreams and wishing that they would go away. I marched into my hallway closet and grabbed my emergency if-I-ever-became-brave-enough-to-go-to-New York City suitcase. The contents of the suitcase included my oversized Miss Honey shades; my favorite play *Seven Guitars* by August Wilson; an old poem I wrote in high school; the first *People Magazine* I had ever purchased, which was almost ten years old; Nans old Bible that contained notes she wrote me on the bottom of her favorite passages; and a sparkling, jaw-dropping evening gown Nan made me promise I'd wear when I accepted my first Tony award. And don't laugh. I know I'm not going to win a Tony on my first real trip to New York. I only packed it for dramatic flair. I did a once over of the house to make sure everything was turned off and in place, and I realized I almost forgot to take out the trash. I walked over to grab the trash and noticed Officer Kendrick's card; it was just sitting there all lonely and soiled from whatever I threw it on top of. I stood there staring at the card and contemplating on it, and that's when I decided to take it out and take it with me and *yes* I know what you're thinking. Would I ever learn? And the answer is *yes*, I will learn, but today was not that day and I also knew nothing was going to stop me from taking that card.

I hit the road feeling high as a kite. I wasn't even bothered by the five stops I had to make to use the bathroom, but I did make a mental note to not drink a liter of water while taking a road trip. This drive was the best two hours of true alone time I had in a long time. I put The Cake Man out of my mind and once I came out of the Holland Tunnel, I started singing "Start Spreading the News, I'm leaving today, I want to be a part of it, New York, New York." My Frank Sinatra rendition was interrupted by the horns blowing and the carefree driving of yellow cabs, zigging and zagging all over West Street. The people were moving fast in large crowds. It seemed as if everyone had something important to do and some defining place to be. New York was loud, fast and smelled of possibility. I'm not sure why I was laughing uncontrollably but I felt like I was home. I pulled over and texted Meredith and Carmen to let them know I was going to stay in New York for a while. I knew if I had informed the girls beforehand that they would try to turn this into a fashion filled girls' trip and I needed some alone time. I called Kirsten to let her know I was here and that if I attempted to find my way to her apartment that I would get lost, so she agreed to come and get me.

So here I was sitting in the car waiting for Kristen to come meet me and out of nowhere I felt as if panic slapped me across the face. I mean my right cheek was actually throbbing. I rolled the window down and tried to get a whiff of some of the New York possibility and then came the doubtful voices. I heard Rece telling me I could not act my way out of a paper bag; I heard my manager telling me to be grateful for my two-percent-a-year raise; I heard myself saying, "You do not have the right to be here."

The panic took over and I U-turned in the middle of the street; the yellow cabs zigged and zagged to get out of my way. I came to a screeching halt because I almost mangled the car in front of me.

"Stop!" I was actually yelling, "Stop! Stop! Stop!" This voice coming out of me was foreign; it was powerful and authoritative and it was mine or at least I think it was.

Wow! This was a voice I never heard before; it was as if I was hearing a new part of me that I never knew existed. Nan would always say that God puts gifts in our bellies and right now I think my gift was unwrapping; I didn't recognize myself. I froze behind the wheel and checked my rearview mirror to make sure it was still me in the car; maybe I had been replaced by an alien host or something. I was having a tug of war in my car with myself. I pulled over again and this time I was facing the Holland Tunnel, while New York, my dreams, and all my courage were at my back and all that was comfortable and normal to me was in front of me. I could call Kristen and tell her I was going to drive back home. I could lie and say I wasn't feeling well. And actually I wasn't feeling well. It hurts to break away from what you know, even if the comfortable known is not good for you. It's still yours and the unknown is so . . . well . . . it's just so unknown. Just as I started to pick up my phone to dial Kristen, it started ringing and of course it was Kristen and thank God. I was just going to run, yes gun it right toward the tunnel and explain later, but again I heard that strong voice, and the warrior came out. I cleared my throat, took a deep breath, "Hello."

"Um hello why are you on the wrong side," the voice answered for me.

"You know that I'm geographically challenged. I'm turning around now."

This time I looked before I turned around and carefully avoided having to call Geico to explain why I caused a pileup in the middle of a busy New York City street. I followed Kristen through the confusing streets of this tough town and then we ended up on Broadway; the lights were bright and bold; the colors blended in with the billboards of *Wicked* and *Chicago*. Each theater production seduced me with the inviting announcements. For a split second I allowed myself to imagine that one of those announcements read, *Starring Athena Davenport.* We finally arrived at 109 Broadway; Kristen and Gary's condo was called the Ansonia, and I was stuck right in front of the large double doors. The door man called out to me twice before I could muster up the nerve to walk through the magnificent doors. It was rumored that celebrities took up residence in this place and for the next couple of weeks I would finally be amongst my own kind—Ok, well my own kind in my head.

Kristen smiled bashfully as she often does and I knew she felt guilty. She always felt guilt over her blessings in life. I'm sure it was a result of our upbringing. I tried my best to conceal my recent heartbreak and I kept the little green-eyed monster at bay. But I couldn't help feeling jealous as our heels clicked and clacked on these gorgeous marble floors. Wow, real marble in the lobby and the crystal chandelier made me feel so small. Kristen held my hand as another door man smiled and ushered us into the elevator and swiped the key for the top floor.

"It's too much, isn't it?" she asked. It was too much for the average person, but Kristen was never average.

"No it's amazing and you know Gary wants nothing but the best for you." I couldn't concentrate on the conversation that I was having with my sister because I couldn't help but wonder, where in the heck was *my* Gary? Did I not deserve one? But then I remembered my mission, I was not supposed to think of a Gary, Peter or a Paul. I needed to focus on my auditions. The elevator doors opened and I got off and became completely undone as I stepped into paradise; this apartment was bigger than any I have ever seen. Kristen and Gary had boxes and bags everywhere; it was clear that they weren't quite settled, but I was family so I didn't mind.

There were five bedrooms in this place—a master bedroom, a guestroom, a meditation room, Gary's office and a no purpose room as Kristen called it. The guest bedroom was decorated in earth tones and I knew that Kristen thought of me. "So this guestroom looks like it screams, 'Welcome Athena." Kristen smiled at me and said "Well, the room was this color when we moved in, so maybe the universe knew you were coming before we did." She gave me another coy smile, blew me a kiss and left me alone with my thoughts. She really is a great little sister.

I opened the large windows in the bedroom, looked out amongst the buildings and dared myself to dream. I stood there for a while and let the breeze wash away my fears. I felt like God was giving me a deep cleanse and when it was done I knew I could be changed. I felt the strong forcing the weak out; I was always in the middle of an internal war with myself. I noticed that I had a built-in shoe closet and I knew I had to bring the girls back to see Kristen's new pad.

I took off my jacket and hung it up and there was Officer Kendrick's card sticking out of my pocket.

Have you ever felt guilt over something that you have not even done yet? I had the card in my hand. I reached for my phone and dialed *67 to block my number and then I dialed the cop's number.

"Officer Kendrick Ryan speaking." I instantly hung up on him. His voice was still kind and warm. I started to wonder what type of man he was and that wondering got me to daydreaming about the types of conversations we could have that may lead to dates and love and, *Oh would you just stop it, Athena!* There was that strong voice again, and again it was loud as if another person were standing right in front of me. After the drive I was exhausted and ready to obey, so I stopped the foolish daydreams about a life with Officer Kendrick, and I climbed in bed, and before I knew it I was fast asleep.

Daniel

I awoke Monday morning just in time to thank Gary for allowing me to stay. It was about 5:30 am and I could smell the dark roast leading me to the cup. I wondered if I had previously mentioned that I love coffee. The granite marble counter tops in this kitchen were fit for a Chef but unfortunately Kristen was no cook, so I'm guessing it was just for show. I paused at the door to watch them embrace; this was the kind of stuff most girls dreamed of and my sister had it. I gently cleared my throat, "Will you two go get a room?"

They both looked up a little embarrassed. Gary smiled at me, "We have a few rooms in this place." And then he said there was no need to thank him for letting me stay. Gary kissed Kristen and playfully bumped my shoulder and left out the door to go make the money.

This was a nice start to the day, sitting in my sister's huge kitchen having coffee and bonding like we did as children (minus the trendy décor). Teresa allowed us to drink coffee as children; it was one of our family things. After our third cup we were both wired. Kristen was off to interview for a new finance manager position, and I was actually hitting the big streets of NYC for my first audition. A few months ago I had joined an actors' group called Back Stage, and they had a website that was a God-send to any hopeful actor. Back Stage housed all the major and minor auditions in all the major cities. The Big Apple was number one on their list, but up until now I never had the nerve to search for anything.

Today, I convinced myself that I was ready to kick Monday's butt; on the outside I roared like a lion as I walked out the large scary doors of the Ansonia, but on the inside this little mouse was dying. I mentally gave myself a pat on the back for even attempting to tackle an actual big city audition. I turned right and headed to the corner and tried my best to hail a cab. Now, I wished I had taken Kristen up on her offer to use Gary's car service, but I didn't want to be a bother. She warned me to leave at least two hours early because she knew I would get lost and that the yellow cabs would be hard to catch. She tried explaining this new app that I could download on my phone and request a ride but I wasn't in the mood for a tech lesson, so I stuck with a traditional cab.

After about 30 minutes I was finally in the back of one, but it felt more like a high speed chase. Once I put on the seat belt, I told the driver I'd like to go to 155 Bank Street Theatre. The driver gave me a naughty once over, nodded his head and slammed his foot on the gas. His once over made me wonder if my black v-neck T-shirt was a little too low cut. I was going for the low key grunge look; I'd read up on the new *it* look for young actors and I didn't want to be too sexy. This driver sped through every yellow light and he even went through a few red lights. I felt nostalgic and even though nothing happened yet, being in the back of this cab was a dream come true. I closed my eyes as an attempt to take it all in and that's when I had a vision of Nan. She was sitting in front of her vanity in her night robe pinning up her curls with bobby pins as she had done so many times before.

She turned to me and said, "Do not let your heart be trouble and do not be afraid". I'm sure this was one of Nan's favorite scriptures, I couldn't figure out which one but it calmed me. I came from a Christian background, but I definitely wasn't the practicing type, so either my Christian card had just been activated or I needed to skip this audition and be dropped off at the Manhattan Psychiatric Center. Before I had time to choose, I could feel the car slowing down, and then we stopped moving. I knew the cab driver was staring at me, but I did not want to open my eyes, and then his thick staccato accent finally interrupted my thoughts.

"Babi, that will be $58.00." For a brief moment I thought he was kidding. How far was this theatre, China? The driver sucked his teeth to show his growing impatience and I knew this was not a joke. At this rate I'd blow through Nan's money by the end of the week. I paid the sexy Caribbean cab driver his $63.00 which was what he claimed I owed plus a tip because I have manners. I stepped out in front of a somewhat modern theatre. The building was a heather grey color and a little worn, but in a good way. I just knew many successful productions happened here. The theatre was considered off Broadway which was a great start for me. I was still standing out front and not moving, trying to act tough and take it all in. I think I did have time for one meltdown or maybe even two because the open call didn't start until 12 pm.

The massive line started to get longer and I wanted to run. Dammit! I had cement feet and I couldn't move; it must have been noticeable because the cutest redhead walked over and whispered in my ear. "Just breathe," he said. Oh my, he was adorable, light freckles dusted his cheeks and those beautiful grey eyes. He looked so familiar to me; his goofy smile put me at ease, and I felt as if I had seen this smile somewhere before. He stretched out his pale, boney hand and introduced himself. And I knew this was my Daniel. He stopped for a second; he recognized me, too; then out of nowhere he hugged me tight.

"Athena, it's me Daniel." He was a student teacher I had met at a beginners' acting class that I attempted to get in years ago at the Walnut Street Theatre in Philadelphia, but I punked out. I remember that day clearly; I was all set to register and then he explained what I should learn by taking his class. Back then the thought of attempting acting made me sick, so I never went back. We kept in touch through texts and quick chats. He always urged me to come back. He said I had that special something, but I never believed him. I always felt like we had a connection and that he wanted more. He was now a technical assistant at the theater here in New York and he was right. I had forgotten to breathe.

It was a true gift seeing Daniel here, and the timing couldn't have been more perfect. I was auditioning for a comedy called "Dirty Thirty." This was a production about a young woman who had a meltdown at work when she turned thirty. Well, wasn't this art imitating life? I started to wonder how many people cracked as they reached Old Man Mountain. I finally stepped in line as number three trillion and patiently awaited my fate. I watched as each hopeful actor sized up the next. Some of the actors were doing voice exercises and making strange native call noises, while others were doing deep breathing techniques and as for me, I was horrified. The closer I got to the front of the line, the more my hands started to tremble. I came prepared with two monologues each under a minute long. I knew them like I knew every word that Noah Calhoun said to Allie in my favorite love story *The Notebook.* I couldn't figure out why the heck I was thinking of *The Notebook.* Damn, I was nervous. Then, I heard a raspy, annoyed voice shout "Next!" I looked around for the next hopeful—Oh Lord the next hopeful was me. I actually started to chant Nan's prayer. I wasn't sure if it would work, but I had to try something to calm myself.

I walked onto the stage and there were five people sitting in the front row. I had Googled how to audition for the first time, so I knew not to let the blinding lights upstage my performance. I had no idea they would be this hot. I could feel the sweat beads forming on the back of my neck. One of the five people in the front row was Daniel. All I could make out was the bright red hair, but his presence made me feel a little less like I was dying. I blew a piece of hair out of my eye and took a deep breath.

"Hello. My name is um." I could barely hear myself speak. I think I was whispering. Damn. I was actually whispering. I had to give myself a pep talk and fast. I said to myself, "You have the right to be here, you have the right to be here." Then I found my voice. I made a mental note to figure out where it ran off to and then I introduced myself.

"Hello, My name is Athena Davenport and I will be doing a piece called 'Seven Guitars' by August Wilson."

"That's it, good girl," I said to myself. And just as I was about to begin, the raspy voice behind the blinding lights asked me if Athena was my real name or my stage name. I was used to people not believing that my mother would actually name me Athena. I smiled as sweetly as I could and answered, "Yes, Athena is my real name." And then I began the piece and to my surprise, I had remembered all my research about auditions.

I felt full of power and range and then the raspy voice said, "Thank you that will be all." I never got to the next monologue; I stood there for a few minutes in shock because that was my best and only performance.

I whispered a meek, "Thank you," and rushed off the stage, spirit crushed, holding back tears. When I opened the door to go outside, the air no longer smelled of possibility but reeked of hopelessness. I didn't even know which way to go, but I was not hailing any more $58 cab rides so I just headed west. I had no sense of direction and my heart was broken; I wanted to go back to Philly. I heard someone calling my name. I turned around to see that it was Daniel. I needed to get away from him, so I started walking really fast, and the walk turned into a sprint, but he kept calling me, so I started to full out run as fast as I could. I was too embarrassed to face him after I was thrown off the stage.

"Athena, Athena," he shouted. I knew he was on my heels, but it sounded like he was right next to me, and once I felt him grab my arm, I knew he was right next to me. What in the heck? Did he train for the Olympics? I finally stopped to face him and the tears broke loose; man was I a mess. Daniel put his head down and relaxed his hands on his knees in an attempt to catch his breath; he was all huffy and puffy and that's when I saw it; he was holding my purse. I was such an idiot; he wasn't trying to talk to me; he was trying to return my purse. I had left it when I rushed off the stage. I reached for my purse; I felt bad that he had to chase me, but all I wanted to do was get away from him. Daniel finally began to catch his breath but he would not let go of my purse and I knew my great escape had come to an end.

"Athena, why are you running away and crying?" He looked generally concerned and confused by my actions. I paused before responding; I needed to make sure his look of concern was genuine and I decided if he chased me for several blocks to return my purse that Daniel was a pretty decent guy and from what I could remember he was kind. So on the corner of 314 West 11th Street, right in front of the trendy restaurant, The Spotted Elephant is where we renewed our friendship. With some reluctance I began to explain the story of how I ended up auditioning at the Bank Street Theatre. I was like an open book. I even spilled the beans about cake man. He searched my face like he was looking for lost treasure. The wind was chilly and he moved a few hair stands out of my eyes. I had forgotten how funny he was, and after a while I stopped thinking about my hurt feelings and just enjoyed the moment.

My stomach began to growl loudly, and he finally asked if I wanted to go inside the Spotted Elephant for lunch. He explained that this place was known for American and Italian food, but in my opinion it had more of a Moroccan feel. The bold colorful curtains made me want to take a crack at belly dancing but only in my mind; there were little brass elephants in strategic places all around the dining area. This restaurant reminded me of how most people think of New York restaurants; hip, trendy and expensive. Once we were seated, I asked Daniel about his life and how he ended up here. He explained that he was born and raised on the Upper East Side of Manhattan and that he took the job at the Walnut Street Theatre because every teaching job was taken in New York and he loved to teach. His upbringing included luxuries like fancy dinner parties, door men, language tutors, and vacations to foreign lands, a penthouse on Park Avenue and a hefty college education from NYU. Daniel was supposed to be a chip off of his dear old dad, a successful shark of a divorce attorney and a part of New York's most elite legal team. After graduating with honors he explained how outraged his father became once he learned that Daniel had his own ideas for life that included the arts and Broadway and not taking the Bar exam.

Our waitress stepped in to take our orders and I was a little confused about the lunch menu; he suggested that I'd go with the char-grilled Kobe Wagyu burger with brie. Daniel continued with his story and eventually our food came. I bit my fancy burger, the best burger I had ever tasted. I quickly shifted my mind off of this perfectly cooked burger and back to his story. He ended the story with his father disowning him, cutting his trust fund and his mother sneaking to help him financially and attending most of his shows. Daniel was one of those people that I discussed earlier that left it all behind and bet on himself. Besides teaching he also ran the technical rehearsals at the Bank Theatre by day and was a part of the who's who of the up and coming theatre *C-List* actors and I was lucky enough to know him. He laughed at my facial expression as the director Mr. Alonzo Rubino interrupted my performance. Daniel said as soon as Mr. Rubino asked me about my name he knew he was interested in me. He also said most newbies don't get that far on his stage.

Daniel's news melted my heart and we spent the rest of the day walking, talking and laughing. Before long, it was getting dark and Kristen started calling to make sure I had survived my first audition. Daniel hailed a cab, but I protested because of my last cab ride. He put me in the back seat, asked for my phone, added his number and quickly slipped the driver some cash before I could object.

He smiled at me and disappeared down the street. The cab ride home was pleasant, nothing at all like the first trip. Daniel was special and I knew this time that I would keep him around, but only as a friend. The driver pulled up in front of the Ansonia and I hopped out of the cab unbothered. I walked straight through the large doors and breezed right through the lobby as if I owned the place. And I gave myself a mental pat on the back for getting through my first audition in NYC.

Day Two

It was Tuesday morning and again I was a slave to the dark roast. I could smell it from the kitchen; as my nose twitched and wiggled. I guessed this would be my wake-up call for the rest of my time here. I could hear Fleet Wood Mac's "Dreams" playing in the distance. I checked my phone and found I had a text from Daniel and a few missed calls from Teresa and the girls. I read Daniel's text and it said, *Day Two.* I rolled over and looked up at the dramatic, cathedral ceilings in the room, there were tiny words infused all over, but I couldn't make them out. Then, I remembered asking Kristen why she had magnifying glasses on the nightstands in the bedrooms, but she said, "You'll figure it out," and I think I just did. This was exciting for a Tuesday morning; it was like hunting for gold. I guess when you have a little money you can create whatever you want in your home. I grabbed the magnifying glass and stood up on the bed. And the words said, *be limitless, be fearless, be free.* I read these words quietly and desperately; then I read them again but fast and hard. I tried my best to push them inside my soul, and my eyes began to water. And that's when I knew Kristen had decorated this room in rebellion against the way we were raised. I jumped down off of the bed and caught a glimpse of myself in the mirror that stood in the corner. I looked a little different, maybe even a little bit stronger and I felt good.

I walked the halls to the kitchen and lightly touched some of the art work hanging on the walls; this place was so alive, it was their very own personal museum. I could hear Kristen and Gary laughing. I had caught them again, but this time they were playfully dancing. I watched and tried not to laugh; her feet could not catch the beat but he never seemed to notice; he couldn't take his eyes off of her. I decided not to bother them, so I backed away without being noticed. I walked to my room and replied to Daniel's text saying *Day Two.*

He immediately called me, "Hey I didn't realize you would be up this early." I explained that my sister and her fiancé' were up this early every morning and that my love for their coffee always woke me with them. Daniel and I chatted for a while and we agreed to meet up after my acting class. I sat the phone on the Victorian nightstand; I had one on each side of the bed, and they reminded me of something that was fit for a queen's quarters. I noticed Officer Kendrick's card; I must have sat it there and forgotten about it.

I'm guessing you know what happened next; I think I was becoming a phone stalker. I was sure this was against the law in some states, but hopefully phone stalking was not illegal in New York.

I dialed *67 to block my number and I called him, "Hello Officer Kendrick speaking," he said. His voice was still warm. "Hello, who is this?" I could tell he was annoyed, but he still sounded so sweet. I giggled, wishing that he knew it was me and I hung up. I was playing with fire; the old me wanted to call him and talk to him; the new me knew better than to call him and the somewhere-in-between me could only dial his number and hang up. ***How many of us change only to turn around and repeat the same action we are delivered from? How is it that some of us still do not know how to be still?*** I started to wonder what or who would be my anchor? Nan would always say, "Without God we blow like feathers in the wind." I shushed my thoughts of her and got ready for the day.

The sun was bright and the streets were noisy and busy; I could smell a mixture of foods from the nearby food carts, and I promised myself to get an authentic New York hotdog before I went home. Although I had only been in New York for one full day, I was already feeling like a true New Yorker. Today I took Kristen's advice and used the car service. As soon as I started walking, the cool air blew my wild hair all over the place. I felt a little silly as I tried to get it back in order so that I could look posh as I walked to the black Lincoln town car. I said, "Hello" to the creepy dude in the men-in-black getup who would drive me. He nodded and I guessed that was my cue to shut up, so I did just that.

I was on my way to the Tree House Theatre; I was taking the only beginners' acting class in New York that I could afford, and the cost was the same price as yesterday's cab ride, so I had taken this as a sign and purchased a ticket late the night before going to bed. After yesterday's audition and Daniel's advice, taking a class just made sense. The car pulled up to a tiny building sandwiched between a Korean barbeque and a nail salon. A small sign on the door said, "Tree House Theatre floor two," In green printing. I wasn't sure if I should get out because it looked a little odd, but then I decided to be brave. The creepy driver advised me that he would be back to get me in exactly two hours, which was perfect timing because the class was two hours long. I nodded the way he did in an attempt to make a joke but he gave me nothing; he just looked at me stoned faced. I decided I'd better hop out of this car before he changed his mind and pulled off with me inside.

I walked upstairs to the second floor and I got slapped by my dear friend panic attack. I tried to stay calm, but it wasn't working, "Oh please panic, I'll hang out with you later, just leave me alone for now." My talk was not working and I was getting dizzy. I really could use a paper bag. Then, I remembered 2 Timothy 1:7, from Nan and I started feverishly chanting this scripture under my breath. "I have a spirit of power, love and a sound mind, not fear or something like that." I knew I was mixing up the words and that I was reaching, but then after a few seconds, my friend panic had actually left the building. This had never happened before. Normally I would need a paper bag or I would need to sit down for an hour. I felt like I had just won the lottery.

"Hello my tall friend." I turned to see a woman watching me; she was the real life version of my Miss Honey. She walked straight up in my personal space and closed my mouth because it was wide open. She went by the name of Pauline; she wore a studded turban, brick red lipstick and a long black kaftan. She had a regal mix of a

British and Jamaican accent. Her skin was tight and perfect; her blond locks hung out of the turban at waist length. She was so poised that I almost bowed; she hugged me tight and I felt fire. Who was this woman of my dreams? I always hear people say Oprah or Taylor Swift is the friend in their head, but I was literally meeting the real friend in my head.

"Well, chile speak," she said.

"Hello I'm Athena and I'm here for the beginner's class."

She laughed loud and said, "Well chile so am I; now come."

She literally dragged me into the class. Wow, this place was amazing; there was a drummer dressed in African attire in the corner; his eyes were closed and his hands seemed to have a mind of their own. The melody was so captivating I started rocking my hips. Then I heard a harmonica in another part of the room from a jiggly, bald, tattooed guy, and I started clapping my hands. I watched a blond beauty command the attention of the other students; she pranced in the circle as each student mimicked her. Pauline nudged me in the circle and before long I had caught on to the exercise and it was my turn. There were no rules, only to step inside of this circle in front of these strangers, to let the melody take you away and to be free. I stepped in with caution and I could feel the heat that each student left behind. I did nothing for a few seconds and then something took me and I was gone. This person in the circle was not the quivering little cub that came here, but she was the queen lioness ready to defend her right to be here. My arms dangled and swayed wildly; I leaped and sang a cry that came from my gut. I swung my head from side to side as if I were possessed with passion. I could see Nan smiling at me and handing me a present, but this time it wasn't Teresa's fear.

I could see Kristen holding my hand, and we opened Nan's gift together, I could see Teresa giving us a new gift. In this circle I was the cause of shedding the family fear and breaking the chains. I sang a melody from the fire in my gut; wow, I didn't even know I could sing this way and I knew that I was meant to be here. I slowly opened my eyes to see the students clapping, and some of them were teary eyed. The circle eventually dispersed and Pauline stepped in and said, "Now Darlings, now we are ready for the script work."

I hit that small stage running and made my character come alive. How was I doing any of this? ***Have you ever had a level of strength come from your core that you never knew was there?***

There is no way anyone could have told me that I would release a level of bondage in a small acting group full of strangers in New York City, but this afternoon that is exactly what I did. As the two-hour class came to an end, I had to thank Pauline. We seemed to be rushing toward each other; we paused and then ended up in a mother and daughter like embrace. Pauline gave me her number and invited me to do personal one-on-one sessions.

She sat there in the moment for a while and just smiled at me, and then she said, "Chile can't you see you got that special something that money can't buy?"

I would eventually come to understand what she meant. I wondered how many other people out there were walking around carrying gold but were living like peasants weighed down by scrap metal. I hugged a few possible friends, locked in a few phone numbers and headed down the stairs. I defiantly stomped past that same spot where I had the panic attack. I felt so free. I opened the front door and there was the man in black just as he said.

He held the door open for me and I nodded, but this time I could care less if he got my humor. I called Kristen to see if she would mind if I did a little sightseeing and I would get dropped off to Daniel.

"Of course you can keep the car for as long as you need, but who is this Daniel guy?"

I could tell she was skeptical and given my track record with dating I didn't blame her. I explained that Daniel was someone I knew from Philly in the acting circle and a real nice guy. I chatted with Kristen about her getting a second interview and her busy day of shopping. The man in black quietly agreed to drive me anywhere my heart desired, and it was no shocker that I wanted to drive past the Broadway theatres.

Wow! I felt alive; my heart danced as we passed the bright lights and scattered playbills on the ground. I closed my eyes to think of that secret dream that scared me; it's the dream that we each tuck deep down inside of that quiet place in our hearts. It's that thing we don't want to tell anyone, but it's also the thing that we are put here on earth to complete. Judging by the way my heart was dancing, my thing wanted out of its quiet place.

The town car pulled in front of a secret dive; there was a large swanky Lucite sign with silver writing on it that said, *John and the James.* New York was known for its many hidden gems and I just happened to get a plus one from Daniel for this place.

I got out and told the man in black I would no longer need his services and he nodded and drove off. Thank God I was dressed well enough to fit in. I learned a long time ago that black is never a miss but always a hit if it is done correctly and tonight I felt classic. However, I was a little sweaty from class so I walked away from the crowd and gave myself a few sprays of *Ladybug* which was a favorite perfume that I always kept in my bag for emergencies.

I waited in the line full of artsy fartsies, possibly high-priced call girls, fashionable grungy actors, suited business men, and then there were the Plain Jane types such as myself. I wore black tight ripped jeans that hugged my curves and a black tank top, black mini leather jacket and black motorcycle boots. I had the wild wavy bed hair courtesy of all the sweating in today's class. Nan's oversized cocktail ring gave me just the right touch of style and I was ready.

During the ride over I noticed that Daniel sent me a text that said, "*Thirteen.*"

The gatekeeper had a stern look on his face as he said, "What's your number honey"? I was so excited about the class that I never bothered to ask Daniel why he sent the text until now.

I reluctantly responded and said, "Number 13."
After my number was approved, another gatekeeper appeared out of nowhere and ushered me into a dark alley and up a flight of chipped stairs that desperately needed a fresh coat of paint. The stairs led to another flight of rotten stairs and finally to an elevator that was guarded by a female gatekeeper that reminded me of a younger version of Dorothy Dandridge.

And again she asked for my number, but this time before I could answer, some guy stepped in and said,

"Her number is 13."

I turned around to see my savior and standing before me was a 5'8", muscular, salt and pepper, mature, sexy and extremely powerful looking man. And judging by the female gatekeeper's reaction he was definitely somebody in this place. She couldn't keep her cool as she giggled and squirmed when she thanked him.

"It's all a numbers game in this place, pretty lady," he said.

There was something so inviting about this man and he smelled of money. Nan would tell us forces are always working against us and sometimes we don't recognize we are being played.

Tonight was the beginning of a setup I never saw coming. The numbers rule in this place was the silliest thing I had ever heard; you couldn't get in without a number and somehow it was attached to your status in this place.

I wondered what Daniel would see in a stuffy place like this, but then the elevator doors opened and my curiosity was satisfied. The powerful stranger guided me out of the elevator by pressing the small of my back and I felt a little weak in my knees. We all know that old saying about women getting in trouble with powerful men and attraction, and I could feel the trouble running through me.

John and the James was an elaborate bar on the top floor of a contemporary hotel in the Meatpacking District. It was rumored to be named after two brothers who were labor workers that got extremely lucky with winning big in a shady game of cards that almost cost them their heads.

The bar was the epitome of old Hollywood glamour. There were black and white photographs of Sammy and The Rat Pack, Marylyn, Dorothy, Audrey, Rita, Billie, Brando and many more of the greats. The staff was dressed accordingly and this explained the beautiful gatekeeper in the elevator.

I could see Daniel waving to me over the crowd and I turned to my new suitor to thank him but before I could walk away he asked, "What's your name?" But for some reason I could not answer.

I hesitated and he leaned in gently, shook my hand and with a sly smile whispered, "What's in a name?"

I was blushing; did this businessman just quote Shakespeare? New York was full of surprises. His handshake delivered a level of electricity through my body. I tried to gain my composure and I remembered the way the gatekeeper behaved in the elevator.

Who was this guy and what did he just do to me? We stood there in the moment watching one another until Daniel saved me.

"Hey are you okay?"

Daniel placed his arm around my neck in a territorial gesture. And the businessman politely backed away. He said his name was Gerald or Big G to his friends and to everyone else it was Sir, Boss, or Mr. Gleason.

I walked back to the table with Daniel and the rest of the number thirteen's. According to the bar's policy the guests were to be seated at the tables with other like numbers. The policy also stated that you had to be personally invited by the owner or a senior staff member and financially healthy enough to afford the lofty bottle service that came with an

80% markup. I guess Daniel must have had his secret trust fund card for the night or used his *C- List* theatre pull to get me in. The head honchos socialized at table number one and unless invited, there was no way to get past the gatekeepers. Table number one was the ultimate VIP experience that came with exotic champagne and hand and neck massages. After that handshake it was hard to concentrate on anything Daniel tried to tell me, nor did I remember to discuss my amazing class.

Daniel was extremely clingy tonight and I felt guilty, so I tried my best to give him my undivided attention. I could feel the music vibrate in my chest; the DJ played a mixture of hip hop and alternative beats over some of the great classics. I stood in one spot and did a little two step; the waitress came around a few times and we ordered a few trendy drinks off of the menu. My favorite was the *Holiday*, named after the great Billie Holiday; it was a fruitful mixture of Clicquot champagne, aged vodka, organic mangos and fresh squeezed orange juice.

I sipped on my *Holiday* but the guilt set in, I was in this place full of pretentious strangers and I was starting to have heart aches. I knew this was probably the last place that I needed to be after the cleanse I had in class. For as long as I could remember I always had an internal connection to doing what's right and I always felt strong internal warnings when I was doing something wrong. I rarely knew how to tap into those feelings and let them be my guide so I would go with the flow; and that was always a bad idea. I could just hear Nan now asking me how long I was going to stay in the maze. I snapped out of my thoughts and rubbed my chest to calm my heart and caught eyes with the businessman. I blushed every time we locked eyes and each time I quickly looked away. Daniel caught him staring too and he seemed annoyed.

"Hey, do you know that guy?"

I explained the elevator situation to Daniel and how he came to my rescue. Daniel smirked and said, "Can you believe him in that overdressed stiff suit"?

Ok this night was not going to end well if I didn't act fast, so I did my best to change the subject and decided to make small talk. "So how were you able to get me in this place?"

I watched Daniel's furry brows rise to the ceiling; his freckles stood at attention and his jaw got so tight I thought it would crack. I knew I said something wrong. I made a mental note to remember that Daniel was a little sensitive. He started to respond but then adjusted his locked jaw and took a few breaths.

"So just because I don't walk around in flashy stiff suits and I still have all my hair, I cannot score a plus one to an exclusive bar?" His voice started to raise an octave. "What am I all washed up?"

Sheesh, this was really going bad; I wanted to enjoy my night, but so far I was doing a real bang up job and I still had those heart aches. I liked Daniel and I thought I should leave before I did or said anything else stupid. I turned to him and pecked him on his cheek.

"Hey, maybe I'm just tired from my class. I'm going to get out of here."

His face instantly softened and I think I saw guilt; he moved a strand of hair out of my face and before he could speak, I turned and walk away. This was supposed to be a celebratory day; my class was amazing and I was in this beautiful place in New York but it just felt wrong.

Has anyone ever felt lonely in a room full of people? I was searching for peace in all the wrong places. Why was Daniel being so weird? Was I sending him mixed signals? I wanted to be kind to him as he was kind to me, but I just wanted to be his friend and I felt awful or maybe I wanted more and I was afraid to explore that.

I quickly bobbed and weaved past the sexy strangers as their dancing and laughter became a blur. I needed to clear my head and get out of this place, but before I reached the elevator the business man grabbed my wrist and pulled me close. And again there was the electric shock; man I really didn't need this right now so I backed away.

"What in hell do you think you are doing"?

I did my best to appear angry but I was actually intrigued.

"Hey I'm sorry pretty lady; you were moving so fast and I tried getting your attention across the room way, way back at table thirteen."

There was something about the way he said "way, way back at table thirteen" and I knew he meant to be mean spirited. He asked why I was leaving so soon, but before I could answer Daniel stepped in and snatched the words out of my mouth.

"Because she's tired and wants to go home."

I snapped my head toward Daniel in annoyance, but I dared not speak a word against him because his facial expression said it all. I turned to the business man; I felt like I was a prized trophy. I repeated what Daniel had just told him, but this guy was tough and was not backing down.

"Ok, well let my car service take you and your guy friend anywhere you want to go."

Man this was awkward, and I thought Daniel was going to go crouching tiger hidden dragon on him. His voice got all high pitched again and screechy as he yelled.

"Friend. Her Friend."

I softy grabbed his hand to calm him and gently responded, "Yes you are my friend."

I introduced them, "This is Daniel and we can hail a cab but thank you for the offer."

The businessman smirked at Daniel and I could almost see something familiar between them. I thought they knew each other.

"We have our own car service, Thank you."

Wow I wondered if everyone in New York had a car service and I wondered if I would ever hire my own. We rode the elevator in silence and once we got outside, he turned to me and seemed like normal Daniel again. I was relieved about his car service because my feet were punishing me. I had been on them for hours.

"Thank God we don't have to hail a cab. I'm kind of tired."

Daniel winced and gave me a look of stupidity and apologized. He explained that he hadn't used his family's car service since he was not in his father's good graces.

Ok, now I was pissed; this was typical classic jealous guy behavior. I was cold, tired, and hungry and my heart ached. Now I wanted to go crouching tiger on Daniel, but instead I let the cold air calm my nerves. We walked side by side for a while without words and this was our truth; we were friends, but he wanted more and I was confused and feeling guilty and still thinking of the businessman.

I told him he could make it up to me by finding me food and listening to me talk about my wonderful day in class. He happily agreed and he gave me the biggest childlike grin. I looked over my shoulder and saw the businessman standing in front of the door watching us as we faded into the early evening. I made another mental note to ask Daniel later about that businessman.

After a large bowl of greasy chicken egg foo young for two and three cups of tea, I was delivered safely back to the front door of the Ansonia. I hugged Daniel goodbye and he held me so tight I thought I would pop. I wiggled out of his death grip; I was starting to get concerned with his behavior, and he really was a good guy. ***Why don't we ever go for the good guys?*** Let's just say the absence of a father in a little girl's life could leave a hole that's so deep she's left searching to fill that craving that no human love can provide. I heard somewhere that defining who you are makes you strong. I was forced to define myself through a series of dating hiccups and a yearning that would not go away. I was starting to feel like I could actually come out of this battle victorious and each day I was a little braver, but I could still feel the old me lingering around like hidden dust, refusing to leave.

I had this unquenchable burning for love; it was the kind of fire that could only be satisfied through quiet time with God but I still had no clue. Daniel was attractive in a sensitive way and he had truthful eyes, so why couldn't it be him. We would eventually spend a lot of time together, it reminded me of when we used to text and talk on the phone for hours which reminded me again to make a mental note to talk with him about just being friends. I had so many mental notes from this day and my head felt heavy. I think I floated up to the top floor because before I knew it I was back in the apartment.

I wanted to tell Kristen and Gary good night, I caught them on the floor praying together in Gary's office; I watched them for a while, and then I started to cry silently. I desperately wanted to join in but there was no way I was interrupting, so I walked back to my room and climbed in bed and fell fast asleep in my clothes.

Day Three

Day three was a blur; after that greasy chicken egg foo young and the drinks, I decided to skip my classes and lounge around the apartment with Kristen. We went through bridal magazines and looked online for venues for her wedding. My sister was a no fuss kind of girl, so for all she cared she could have gotten married at a church and had close friends and family over for dinner. Gary's mother was a different story and she would not have it. Gary's mother was Eartha Kit and Maya Angelou all wrapped into one person. She reminded me of sugar and spice. She dropped by unannounced to remind Kristen she wanted her to book The Hudson River Winery for the ceremony.

Everything about this tiny powerhouse of a woman screamed *money*. Mrs. Gary's mom was a self-made business woman she owned several hotels in different states. She came equipped with a list of stylists, bloggers and anyone else she needed at her beck and call. I could tell she scared Kristen, but she still put her stamp of approval on the engagement.

"Krissy," she said, "We are going to have to get you use to the finer things in life."

Well that was rude! I also noticed my sister fidget in her chair because she hated being called Krissy. I decided to stay out of it and concentrate on extending my stay because there were a few classes that I wanted to take and soaking up the New York way of life was on my mind.

Gary's mom eventually left but the uppity air lingered behind. Kristen and I jokingly ordered food in a snooty tone of voice and marked the dresses we liked. We went through so many magazines and websites my eyes were experiencing a white out. Kristen had that goofy wild look on her face and I knew something was about to happen.

"Gary's mom is wrong. I am use to the finer things in life, and I have a mighty finer-thing in life surprise for you."

My stomach did flips in excitement as I watched her dial a special code on her home phone and just like that the living room was transformed into a spa. Wow! I really could get use to this. I was not going to argue with the royal treatment. Thirty minutes later a whole team showed up in the apartment and I had a fresh facial, mani/pedi and a massage. I was so relaxed from the massage that I found myself in bed laughing at Daniel's text messages; he always did make me laugh. I laughed myself to sleep and I didn't get any work done but day three was amazing.

Day Four

Day four began just like day one, two and three except I woke up bloated from the take out. I peeled my clothes off, threw on some sweats, splashed cold water on my face, and let the coffee lead the way. To my surprise Kristen was alone and she seemed to be in deep thought.

"Hey Giraffe," I said.

I smiled and hugged her. Giraffe was a name that we were given in high school for being so tall, but she was a second taller than me so the name stuck with her. She had been up trying to map out a plan to hold educational meetings for finance repair for impoverished women in the community. She hit a bump in the road because New York was larger than Philly and she didn't know where to begin.

Gary slept in late today and we spent the rest of the morning drinking coffee and trying to solve her geography problem. I had an audition this afternoon and I convinced Kristen to go with me; we planned to do some shopping afterwards. After four cups of coffee and a few hours on Google maps, she finally had her starting point and I had the jitters; we parted ways to get ready for the day.

Normally, I would pace the floor and give myself a power speech about how I was going to crush this audition. But this time I decided to talk directly with God as I chose my audition outfit. I wondered if it was okay to have an informal conversation with the creator of heaven and earth, but I needed something more than my normal pep talk. I think I really needed a friend.

Nan said she would talk to God while she was getting ready in the morning, so I stepped into the closet and grabbed my pair of dark denim ripped jeans and I held them up to the ceiling.

"God, do you think I should go for denim or leggings for this audition?"

I imagined him smiling at me as a father would with his daughter, and he nodded toward the denim, so I thanked him and went with the denim.

"I want you to know that I'm nervous and if you don't mind, could you please show up today?"

I wanted to say so much. I wanted to talk about things that had nothing to do with the audition. I felt a little silly imagining this conversation with God, but then I sensed this strong presence and I knew that I was not alone. In an instant all of my fear was gone; it was like something hit the mute button on all the doubtful thoughts that constantly flooded my mind.

"God is that you?" I said in a terrified voice.

My hands began to tremble and I started sobbing, but this time it wasn't out of pain. Something was happening to me. I could hear words being spoken to my heart, but it did not make sense. How was I hearing words in my heart? The words penetrated that bruised placed that normally caused me so much pain but this time I was full of so much bliss and I could not explain it. The words were like songs and the melodies were indescribable, but if I had to describe it; I would say that if love had a sound then I think this would be it.

Then I started to hear whispers.

"I'm always with you," and then again, "I am always with you."

I'm sure it was the same whisper I heard the day I met Rece on the roof top, but I thought it was the Riesling so I ignored it. I dropped to the floor with the jeans still in my hands and I just sat there. What was going on in Kristen's closet? Was I losing my mind or finding it?

I wrapped my arms around myself, but it felt like the arms belonged to another. Were these God's arms? I had so many questions. The voice finally stopped and I could hear Kristen calling me, but I couldn't move to answer her. She was standing next to me yelling my name and finally she yanked my arm. "God, Athena are you ok?"

I was yanked out of my place of peace. I wanted to slap her but I knew she would not understand where I was. I barely understood where I was.

"Yes I'm fine," I answered.

I explained to her that one minute I was looking for an audition outfit and the next thing I knew I was on the floor sobbing. She looked so worried and I could tell she was forcing a smile; I knew she thought I was losing it.

"Athena maybe it's just the pressure of these auditions which by the way you missed today."

It was already two in the afternoon. Apparently she and Gary ran out to do a quick errand; she thought I was rehearsing and didn't want to bother me. She said she called my cell four times to tell me that she would just meet me after the audition, but she needed the address.

I never heard my phone ring; how could I have stayed on this closet floor for four hours and in the same position when it only felt like a few minutes to me? The last time I saw my sister it was 10 am and we were getting ready for the day. I wanted to tell Kristen everything that happened but I didn't have the nerve. I knew the only person that would understand this would be Nan; gosh I wished I could talk with Nan. I mustered a fake smile for Kristen.

"Yes I promise I'm fine, maybe you're right it was just the pressure."

Kristen pulled me up off the floor and gave me a hug and left me to get ready for our shopping day.

Gerald and the Lamb

I was dressed for comfort and of course I went with the ripped jeans that God suggested. Kristen and I were headed to the Mecca of all shopping districts, Madison Ave. It was nice to spend time with her and we decided on Barney's. I knew there was nothing I could afford on my salary, so I dipped into my stash from Nan and set myself a small limit. Barney's oozed of fancy. Every high-end designer known to man was housed in this palace. The expensive fragrances invaded my nostrils without warning; this was so exciting.

I imagined myself as a loaded, successful actress sashaying through the different departments. I started playing around extending my fingers in a diva-like manner and I could hear Kristen behind me.

"Yes madam you are fab."

But then a deeper voice interrupted Kristen's.

"Yes she really is, fabulous."

We were shocked and we quickly turned to see the businessman admiring me as I imitated the life I dreamed of. He looked so professional and powerful; he wore another dark grey suit almost identical to the one he wore the day we met. He stepped within inches of my face; apparently this guy never learned the personal space rule as a child. I had to take at least three steps back to get some distance between us.

"So do you frequent this place?" I asked.

He gave me a smirk; damn he knew I was nervous.

"Well, no but my personal shopper does."

He said she was away on maternity leave, so he was left to shop for himself. Kristen let off a phony cough and cleared her throat.

"Uhh hum!" Kristen said. She sternly turned to him and introduced herself. I knew that look all too well; she felt like he was trouble and for some reason so did I. This felt like Antonio all over again and what was with me bumping into men when I was shopping.

He paused for a moment and studied our faces and then he said, "Twins."

Kristen sarcastically smiled and mumbled underneath her breath, "Big shocker there genius." I tried my best not to laugh at her.

Kristen headed up to women's shoes, and I told her I'd meet her there in a second. I wanted to say goodbye to the business man.

"Well it was nice seeing you again, enjoy your day."

He cocked his head and gave me a crooked grin. "Hey pretty lady, I'll keep you company while you shop for shoes."

I didn't think he was going to take no for an answer, so I nervously agreed. We chatted about my original reason for coming to New York, and he said he knew a few heavy hitters in the acting industry. It turned out Gerald the businessman was one of the owners of *John and the James*; he'd inherited the place from his father and uncle, and he joked and said all the rumors were true. He owned prime real estate on the Upper East Side and a few restaurants.

The businessman was charming and sly; every woman in Barney's blushed and batted their lashes as we walked past. Every salesman stood at attention as if he were a Sergeant Major in the Marine core. Kristen and I tried on so many pairs of shoes my fingers were getting spasms from all the strapping, lacing and pulling.

Gerald asked the sales girl to bring me a few of his favorite pairs. This strange request made Kristen giggle. She whispered, "Gary hates shoe shopping with me, I might like this guy, after all."

A man who knew his shoes and power suits could be dangerous; this was going to go all wrong. Kristen tallied her damages at the register and I got a flash of guilt for spending Nan's money, so I decided against buying those gorgeous $660.00 pair of *Saint Laurent* pumps. I gently caressed the heel and promised myself that once I landed my first real gig, I'd come back for them. My thoughts of owning my very first pair of red-carpet-ready pumps were interrupted by Gerald.

"Aren't you going to get these?"

Now, I wasn't about to tell this man I couldn't afford them, so I had to think fast.

"Oh no these babies would kill my feet, but they are gorgeous."

I was basically salivating over the heels, so I calmly put them back on the display and tried to play it cool.

He would have bought my story until Kristen walked up and blurted out that she would put them on her charge for me. Gee thanks Kirsten, what a way to embarrass me, I thought.

I smiled with the deer-in-headlights look and said, "Aww no I can buy them, but the heels would kill my feet."

Kristen looked confused and said, "What are you talking about? We owned heels higher than this in high school."

Ok, now I was caught in a lie. I yanked Kristen by the arm and told the businessman good-bye.

I rushed her out of the shoe department, past the cosmetics and fancy dresses and finally I could see the front door. I basically threw her through the doors and we were back on the streets. The town car was there waiting for us, but before we could get in, a tall serious looking man in a suit blocked our way. This guy looked mob scary and we knew he meant business. Kristen and I stood there in confusion; we definitely didn't steal anything, so what was going on?

He mumbled something in his ear piece that sounded a little like *sir yes sir*. "Ma'am it appears that there is an issue with your card; now please head this way." We tried to explain that we didn't own any Barney's cards and that this was a mistake, but this guy would not budge.

We were escorted back to the women's shoe department where an eager platinum blond sales girl awaited our arrival. She grinned from ear to ear and handed me two bags and explained that Mr. Gleason--as in Gerald Gleason as in the businessman--had purchased two gorgeous pairs of shoes for me. I was bewildered, why would he do this? He didn't even know me. I tried to take them back; I even told the sales girl I barely knew him and of course he was nowhere to be found.

Kristen looked skeptical and just as shocked as I was. I stood there thinking about my next move, but then the blond offered to take them off my hands; she shrieked in excitement; she said we wore the same size. I reluctantly handed them over to her, but there was something about watching her get all giddy over my shoes that sparked my self-entitled attitude. I politely peeled her fingers off of my bags, thanked her and headed for the entrance.

The ride over to lunch was awkward. I could feel Kristen's judgmental gaze on me and yeah, yeah I knew I swore off men, but they kept coming. Maybe this was a sign to get back into the game and yes I knew that technically it didn't seem as if I had ever left the game, but something about me was changed.

And I also knew God was trying to tell me something, but at that time I could not hear him. I gazed out the window in deep thought over my closet experience; what did it all mean? Was it even real or did the pressure get to me? *Has anyone ever had a personal encounter with Christ?* I mean isn't this what I needed and what Nan had prayed for? I wanted relief from the heartbreaks and I wanted to accomplish my dreams, so why did it feel like I was fighting the change I said I wanted.

I felt like my insides were being rearranged and it hurt, but I think it was the good kind of hurt; does this make sense to anyone? I shifted my thoughts to my new shoes and the electricity I felt for the businessman.

I was all ready to face Judge Judy so I looked at my sister and she finally broke the silence. "Okay who is Daddy Warbucks and how did we meet him?"

I laughed at the Daddy Warbucks reference. "Well his name is Gerald Gleason and I don't know him; I met him at a lounge with Daniel."

Kristen intently listened and then she said, "Athena do you remember when Nan would tell us to beware of the wolf in sheep's clothing?" Her words punched me in my gut.

I felt like I needed to defend myself, "Are you the only one that deserves happiness little sister?" She looked hurt and I knew I should not have said that.

"Athena you're older by a few minutes and it's your life."

Thank God she let me have this; she really could be a stickler when she wanted to be. We decided to open the boxes; there were two beautiful pairs of shoes. The pair I tried on and another pair he chose for me. A number written on a card was taped on the inside of the box that he chose for me; something told me to throw the lid out of the window, but I didn't want to contribute to New York's litter problem, so I closed the box for safekeeping.

We pulled up to a soul food place called Manna's on Lennox Ave; it took us forever to get there. This placed reminded me of Philadelphia and thank God because I was in the mood for more down-to-earth food. I could smell the sweet yams from the door and my stomach started to growl. I tried to hop out of the car, but Kristen pulled me back in the seat and said, "You really should be careful. Something is not right with this guy." She just couldn't help herself and I knew she was right, but I chose not to respond and we headed into Manna's to eat.

This place was so soulful. the people were an eclectic array of women rocking natural afros, bantu knots, trendy blonds in bobs, brunettes in ballerina buns with Jlo inspired hoop earing's, older women in hippie Woodstock dresses and men in vintage leather jackets; some had spiked hair cuts and others had big beards that looked full of wisdom. I'm not sure if I was more excited about the food or the people watching, which was something Kristen and I liked to do. I could hear afro-jazz music playing all through the restaurant and the color schemes perfectly matched the fall weather. It was crowded, so it took a while to be seated; we walked to the bar and ordered sweet corn bread and sweet tea while we waited. We eavesdropped on a conversation that a couple of thirty something women were having. The ladies were talking about how there were no good men left, so they decided to just give up. I thought about how many other women were so close to throwing in the towel on love. I wanted to chime in, but I didn't want to seem nosey so I just listened.

After about forty five minutes, we were seated. We sat and smiled at everyone staring at us because we were twins. We finally ordered lunch and chatted about the venue Gary's mother suggested, the adjustment to New York life and how much we both missed Nan. This food was so good we ordered another round of smothered turkey chops to share and more sweet tea.

Kristen asked me if I thought there were no good men left, and I paused for a moment to search for my true answer. "Yes there are good men left, you have one."

She looked relieved by my answer; although I came into this world first she always seemed worried about me. I'm starting to see that it was easier for us to say there were no good men out there instead of admitting that we were attracting exactly what we say we don't want. *Was it easier to hide within our own insecurities which were direct results of our dating choices?*

Nan use to say, we are all broken pieces of God's puzzle and all he wants to do is make us whole. Facing my truth was something I was not prepared to do in the middle of

Manna's, but I was starting to see that these fractured hearts had everything to do with us and nothing to do with them. Now I'm not saying that the people that hurt us bear no responsibility for their selfish actions. But I will pose this question: ***What do we really think about ourselves? And no, I am not talking about the generic answers we usually give. But why do we freely give our hearts to the undeserving.*** I knew what my thing was, but I carefully had it hidden in my dark place. I also felt like God had been trying for years to show me the light. After lunch we rode back to the apartment full of laughs and tears reminiscing about the good old days.

I decided that today was a good day even though I missed my audition; at least it ended with new shoes and great conversation. Once I was back, I called Daniel. I don't think I heard the phone ring before he picked up.

"Hello, hi is everything ok? Are we okay? Are you ok? I'm really, really sorry about the way I behaved the other day. I couldn't get a word in. He reminded me of one of those fast talking auctioneers so I interrupted him.

"Hey slow down there and 'Yes we are okay."

Daniel explained that he signed us up for an impromptu class the next morning and then we'd do lunch."

I was actually relieved. "Daniel this sounds like a great idea, and it beats my sci-fi dinner theatre audition."

He teased me about my latest audition, but it was all I could find on a Wednesday afternoon as an unknown actress without an agent. I was really looking forward to this class and spending more time with Daniel; after we talked I felt better about our friendship.

As I looked around this gorgeous room, I felt a little sad that this was not my everyday reality. I scooted to the edge of the bed and my eyes landed on my new shoes. I sat there for a while and watched them; were they going to grow legs and run out of the door? I wished they would have; it would have been less trouble for me if those shoes had just walked themselves right out the front door and never came back. I knew that wasn't logical thinking, so I opened the box that I picked out first; I put them on and started prancing around and I felt like a runway model.

I walked to the far end of the room to get away from the other pair. I began to hum under my breath to distract myself from the fact that I wanted to open that other box, and I started moving closer to it.

Athena why are you beating around the bush, I asked myself. I got closer and closer and closer and then I was back where I started so I flung open that box to get to his number.

I dialed his number and got the shock of my life when she answered all bubbly and bright, "Hello Tiffany Nicole speaking."

I wanted to laugh at her name but I knew better, so I introduced myself.

"Oh yes it's you, the Indian giver." She sucked her teeth and I thought she would hang up on me.

I apologized and explained that I had the wrong number. I could tell by her tone that she was still upset with me.

I guess she was still sore about me taking the shoes from her.

"Let me guess; you are looking for Mr. Gleason's number, aren't you?"

I felt like a fool; she had pulled my card, or I guess I can say *I pulled hers*. She went on to say that she left her number in the box just in case I changed my mind about the shoes. Whoa, Tiffany Nicole really wanted my shoes.

"I just want to thank him," I said.

She giggled and in a snarky tone, "I bet you do."

After a few seconds she put me on hold. She said she had his card, and she gave me his number and quickly hung up. I was outwitted and insulted by Tiffany Nicole. I wanted to call her back and tell her I was not that kind of woman, but I was too distracted by the 212 number I was staring at.

As soon as I dialed the number that same electricity I felt at *John and the James* ran through me; man what kind of voodoo was this? Okay I'll just call him to thank him and be done with it. I was laughing at myself because I knew that wasn't the truth.

I was swept by a rush of emotions. First there was the cautious warning; then there was the anxiety; then excitement; then lust and finally guilt. I was guilty because I already knew that the wolf would devour the little lamb and maybe that closet experience could have been deliverance. I dialed his number and I felt weak.

He was not waiting on my call like Daniel because I let the phone ring four times and just as I was about to hang up, he answered.

"Mr. Gleason speaking." His voice was powerful. I searched for kindness and sensitivity, but they were nowhere to be found.

My stomach twisted into knots, so I hung up on him. I knew hanging up was the best decision, but the senseless girl in me could not help herself, so she defiantly reached for the phone. She was now in control, and she was going to answer this phone and no one was going to stop her. I took a few breaths and tried to regain some self-control; he was calling back so this time I let the phone ring four times to teach him a lesson. On the fourth ring I picked up and said *hello* to a dial tone. I couldn't believe that he hung up. I was sure he heard me say *hello*.

I dialed the number again, and my fingers were trembling and my mouth was dry; he answered this time.

"Mr. Gleason speaking."

I was quiet for a second and then I spoke. "Hello Mr. Uh, Uh, Uh, I mean Gerald."

Was I actually about to call him Mr.? Get a grip Athena; you can handle a conversation with a rich distinguished possibly pompous businessman. I could have sworn I heard him growl as he said my name. I closed my eyes and imagined him growling my name; oh this was bad. Hadn't I had my peace of mind? Was my heart not healed? Wasn't I becoming my own hero? I mean after all I did make it to New York.

I was making up excuses as I searched my heart for a reason to give myself permission to talk with him, but surprisingly I could not find one. What was wrong with something as innocent as a conversation? The problem was all forbidden conversations started out innocently. He was no good and I knew this in every fiber of my being but I went against every bone in my body and opened a door that should have never been opened.

"Hello Athena," he growled. "Did you like your shoes?"

Oh yes the shoes; —that's why I'd called him; I stood up and paced the floor, but I purposely avoided the closet.

"Yes thank you for the shoes." I wasn't about to take one step near the sacred closet, so I walked back toward the bed.

He dominated every part of the conversation. I tried to thank him for the shoes and hang up, but he insisted that he see me in them.

"I bet your legs look amazing in those shoes," he said.

I smiled uncomfortably. "I guess they look okay." I hadn't even realized that I had taken off the shoes that I picked out and had put on the shoes that he purchased. I felt sexy and aroused in these shoes and this was real bad.

Athena hang up, please hang up, my mind was shouting at me, but my body was starting to relax.

"Baby nothing about you is just okay." We had only been on the phone for a few minutes and he had already asked to see me twice. I started to get comfortable with his boldness. He barked a few orders at someone as I was placed on hold, and I started to wonder about his lifestyle and how many people's lives he was in charge of.

"Hey, have you ever had fresh caught lobster drizzled in truffle butter?"

But before I could answer he said, "Of course you haven't."

I should have been offended, but I was still trying to figure out what the heck truffle butter was; I really needed to get to New York more often. He demanded that I be ready in the front lobby at 8 pm sharp for dinner. I was told to be clad in a black dress and the shoes he purchased. I was wondering what lobby I was supposed to meet him in.

 "Gerald, are you going to tell me what lobby we are to meet in?"

 He laughed and said, "The Ansonia of course." Then he hung up.

I stood there with the phone still up to my ear with my mouth wide open. How the heck did he know where I was staying? Ok this guy was interesting and maybe a little creepy. I made a mental note to let Kristen and Gary know who he was just in case.

I rushed down the hall and knocked on my sister's bedroom door; she was lying across Gary's lap and they were watching football. I laughed loud at the sight of this. If I knew my sister as well as I thought I did, she was faking because she hated football. Gary looked up and asked what was so funny, but Kristen shot me a look, so I blamed it on my date night excitement.

Gary looked at me in a quizzical manner and asked, "What, are you laughing at your sister trying her best to understand football?" We both started laughing at her and she lunged at me with a pillow.

"Okay, okay I call a truce and especially because I need to borrow one of your fanciest black dresses."

Kristen turned into Judge Judy and gave me the third and fourth degree until Gary rescued me by picking her up and tossing her back on the bed. I left them wrestling on the bed and I headed for my sister's closet or mini mall as I should call it. My sister had the MTV cribs' kind of walk-in closet and it felt like it was a mile long.

She had so many black dresses, I had to play "Eeny, meeny, miny, moe" just to choose one. Some of the dresses were still in garment bags and boxes were still on the floor.

If she didn't hire someone soon, I would help her unpack everything. I settled for the breathtaking knee length strapless sweetheart top.

My heart started to race as I thought about his reaction, but my excitement was interrupted by Kristen's gaze; she had snuck away from Gary and she was eyeing me as I chose a dress. Her look caused a pain in my chest and I wanted to get away from her.

"WHAT are you looking at? Just say it and get it over with."

 But she said nothing and that was worse than one of her judgmental pep talks. I wanted to explode, but I didn't have time; I mean who did she think she was? This was my life.

Have you ever lashed out at someone for exposing something that you knew you had no business doing?

 Well, this is how our nonexistent conversation was going because she would not talk to me but only stare. I marched myself past her and whispered a *thanks for the dress*; I waved bye to Gary who was back in his football trance and ignoring both of us. The walk back to the room felt like the green mile of shame; the shame that I thought was lifted was back and this time it was back with a vengeance.

I felt heavy but I was still going on this date, and at this point I could not figure out why. I hummed under my breath the entire time I was getting dressed to distract myself from unwanted thoughts. I didn't want to think about the closet or why I should not go on the date. I just wanted to go.

I tried my best to press my wild curls. I rarely did this but I wanted to look sophisticated for him. I was surprised to find that my hair hung sleek in place right in the middle of my back; this was going to be a good date. I was clad in my black dress and the purchased pair of *So Kate's* in nude covered my feet. I guess I wasn't lying back at the department store; my feet were killing me, I guess I had to get used to fancy shoes. But tonight I was going to grin and bear it.

I sauntered through the lobby with my coat in my hand. I felt like showing off a little. It isn't every day that I felt confident enough to have all eyes on me. Before I reached the door I group texted Kristen and Gary and gave them Gerald's full name, number and the lounge he owned.

I paused to collect myself. Now I was ready to put on my coat and walk out the door. I watched a black Mercedes Benz that was parked in front of the door, but I was unsure if that was him. It was 8 pm on the dot.

I started to text him but then he said, "Beautiful, you're late."

I turned around to see him standing there watching me. I know I wasn't late; but before I could speak he walked into my personal space again and this time I could not step back because he held the small of my back and I felt that same electricity—it was black magic.

He said that if a person is given an exact time, it is always smart to show up fifteen minutes early. Um, yes for a job interview, I thought to myself but not a date; sheesh this man had a lot of rules. He held my hand and escorted me over to the car and opened the door for me. I got in and we were on our way.

The car was full of pulsating energy, and it was as if our conversations were alive. Nan would always tell us that words have power, so be mindful of how you use them. He sat close to me and nuzzled his nose in my neck.

"You smell lovely. What is that?"

I couldn't think of what perfume I was wearing and then I started to panic. Oh crap, I forgot to put on perfume and I didn't have *Lady Bug* with me.

What could I say? Think fast, Athena. "Um it's soap."

He laughed out loud which put me at ease and I realized that he did have a softer side.

"So tell me something about yourself that you have never told anyone."

"Hmm, something about myself that I never told anyone."

For a second I thought about telling him about Miss Honey but thank God that second quickly passed.

"Umm, I'm afraid of Koala Bears, I'm not sure why because I have never seen one up close and personal but it's just something about those claws that freak me out."

He laughed hard and loud, he couldn't control himself and I couldn't help but watch him because he seemed so free. The rest of the car ride was full flirtatious giggles, light-hearted conversations and me trying to sound sophisticated.

 We arrived at a modern apartment building near Lennox Avenue and my curiosity was high. I could hear my heart beating in my ears. I noticed the same kind of polite doorman that worked at the Ansonia. Once we got out of the car, we were greeted but this building was totally different. For starters the front desk staff and the concierges were Barbie-doll-like women; they wore black dresses and pearls draped around their necks. Nan gave Teresa an authentic pair of pearls, so I could spot a knock off and these pearls were no knock offs.

Everyone stalked our every move as we walked through the front door. We were escorted by two huge men in suits using walkie-talkies to communicate with the other staff members. We entered a glass elevator and I got a full view of the building. Wow! It was breathtaking. I noticed the advertisements on the elevators said *Gleason Enterprises*.

He must have noticed my expression so he leaned in and said, "Yes, she's all mine."

He looked proud and haughty. We rode the elevator to the twenty-first floor, and I braced myself as the doors opened. I stepped into utopia, and I instantly knew this was a false sense of what I experienced back in the closet. I followed him into this beautiful place; even though I felt internal danger, something had me bound in the present moment, and I wanted to keep going. *Are you smart enough to recognize when you are being set up but too broken to stop it? We want what we want, right?*

The restaurant was called *Peixe* which means fish in Portuguese. I asked him, "Why Portuguese?" and he said after experiencing every part of the culture in Portugal one would never be the same. I made a mental note to visit Portugal. *Peixe* was surrounded by glass and even the floors were glass. I could see an alluring pool beneath us surrounded by calming white lights. I could also see the entire skyline from up there and our beautiful server couldn't take her eyes off of Gerald.

"I hope this is to your liking. I closed the entire place for us."

I didn't know what to say. I had never dined that way. The iron tables had hidden jewels encrusted in the edges. He handed my coat to the server; he pulled out my chair and gestured for me to sit. We sat there for a moment, but he never took his eyes off of me.

"Would you like a glass of wine?"

I guessed one glass wouldn't hurt, but before I could ask for Riesling, the server returned to the table with a G-Max 2009 bottle of Riesling by Weingut Keller; she poured the gold liquid in our glasses. I was impressed but curious as to how he knew my favorite wine. I felt he already knew me.

He smiled and said, "This is claimed to be the most expensive wine in the world." Sheesh, I was afraid to swallow it. I coughed a little and again he laughed out loud.

"I'm so glad that I amuse you."

He shook his head, "No it isn't mockery Athena; there is something so pure about you that I want to bottle it and hide it just for myself."

Whoa, this guy was too intense. I was in the most elegant restaurant I had ever stepped foot in, drinking a glass of the world's most expensive wine with a distinguished charmer and I couldn't shake the feeling of displacement. I was never meant to know him or share this moment with him. I thought I really should go back to that closet. I tried my best to enjoy the date, so I sipped my fancy Riesling. I caught him watching me; he asked about my plans for tomorrow and suggested that we charter a jet to anywhere I wanted to go. The thought of chartering a jet disarmed me, and I coughed again and out came the Riesling flying across the table.

I noticed his anger as he summoned the server who urgently appeared with cloth wipes to clean his suit and the table. She must have annoyed him because he slapped at her hand, and she jumped and scurried away; he took a few deep breaths and then looked up at me with a smile but those eyes of his were anything but happy. I apologized, but he waved his hand and smiled again.

"It's okay Athena. Mistakes happen."

He was so focused on my plans. I told him I was meeting my friend Daniel, but the mention of Daniel's name caused his fingers to twitch. He became distant and a little dark; his darkness wasn't outright as his eyes pierced me, but I made a mental note about it because I felt a little frightened.

The lobster dinner interrupted our conversation and his gaze and I finally got to experience truffle butter, and yes he was right. I had never eaten fresh-caught lobster or anything besides regular butter. I had a nice ten-pound gut buster lobster but I held my composure in front of him. This Riesling was so strong that I didn't need another glass. I was tipsy and it seemed as if that's what he wanted.

Once we finished dinner, the two oversized suits escorted us back to the elevator and back through the lobby and again we received the same stares. We got into the car and he sat in my personal space and began to rub my legs which made me quiver. We drove for a while and I think we were heading out of the city; I read a sign that said the Bronx. I thanked him for dinner.

"I really need to get home. I have to be up early." And again I noticed that dark gaze, but he plastered on a smile and asked the driver to pull over.

He paused for a second; he wasn't used to hearing *no*. "Listen pretty lady, a friend of mine owns a private social club in the Riverdale section in the Bronx."

I was full of Riesling and he wanted to take me to this private club. My heart felt heavy in this moment. I wondered what would await me if I joined him. I felt the weight of life and death in my decision. He smirk at me as if he knew my answer and just as I was about to choose death, my phone beeped.

I had a text message from Daniel reminding me about setting my alarm for class and once again I believed that God stepped in. My insides danced and I turned to the businessman and asked him to take me home. His jaw clenched, but again he smiled and signaled to his driver to turn around. I was headed home and I was excited about it. He walked me to the large double doors of the Ansonia and he spoke to the doorman by name. He seemed eager to please and smiled at us. We stood there, so close I could feel his breath in my nostrils and then we kissed.

I couldn't control these exchanges that were taking place as we kissed and I knew these seeds that were planted would come back to me. I ignored the warning to get away from this man and I would eventually reap something I never meant to sow.

I walked through the lobby feeling a little confused. I mean I felt like I should be happy because I had this amazing, successful, powerful man wanting to spend time with me but there was that good ole internal warning that I could not shake and this time it was stronger than the others. I think he was trying to take all of me and if I wasn't careful I'd let him and loose myself.

I was back in the apartment, and Kristen greeted me in the hallway with a cup of tea.

"Hmm were you waiting up for me?" She was caught red handed and she knew it.

"No I was making myself some tea and I didn't want to be rude, so I made you a cup."

I accepted the tea; I could smell lavender in it and after a few sips I started to feel like myself again. We sat in the dining room drinking tea, listening to the grooves of Esperanza Spalding and going over the details of my date. She looked just as amazed as I felt when I tried explaining the details of the jewel-encrusted tables, or the fact the he owned the entire building. I couldn't help but notice her concerned glances as I used my best acting skills to describe how sweet and amazing Gerald was.

Chamomile lavender tea always made me feel cozy and warm, so after I discussed the size of the lobster, I decided to save the rest of the details for another day. I retired to my room and peeled off Kristen's *LBD*. I already had the shoes in my hand they looked incredible but my toes were throbbing. I took a few deep breaths and stood in front of the closet; I couldn't believe I felt nervous to walk into the closet. Somehow I found the courage to walk in and grab a pair of sweats. I was expecting to be swept to the floor; I was expecting to see a great white light or hear that beautiful small voice, but instead there was nothing; well nothing except the smell of lavender tea and wine on my breath, but I felt nothing.

I was alone in the closet which in most cases should be normal, but this didn't feel normal. I felt alone and that made me nervous. Had God left me? Nan said that there is nothing we can do that will snatch us out of the hands of God, so I tried my best to remember that. I put on the sweat pants and my favorite raggedy t-shirt. I sat on the closet floor waiting. I waited and waited and then I waited some more but my eyelids felt like boulders and I started to feel myself falling asleep.

I walked over to the bed, climbed in and let sleep take me away. I was so exhausted; I think I did drift for a few moments but then I felt a gust of wind; man it was freezing. I sat up because of the uncomfortable chill and my first thought was that I had left the window open or maybe Gary had forgotten to pay the heating bill. I was still groggy, so with one eye open I hopped out of bed to close the window and stepped in a puddle. I thought I had knocked over my cup of tea, but I couldn't remember if I had taken it with me or if I had left it in the dining room. My sweat pants were soaking wet and I could feel the water rising above my waste. Ok now I had both eyes open and I was instantly gripped by terror; there was a paralyzing panic slowly rising with the water.

I realized I was standing in the middle on an ocean. I could see frozen ice and water for miles and miles; there was nothing but water all around me. My mind started racing; was I dying? Was this death? Did Nan lie? Did God leave? The wind was howling and the sky felt wicked and dark. I tried to focus and that's when I heard them; I could hear screaming coming from every direction.

"HELP, HELP, PLEASE HELP." I noticed thousands and thousands of women and they were drowning. Some of them were already going under and some were trying their best to stay afloat with their arms stretched towards me.

"Help Athena," they screamed. It was so frantic; my mind raced for answers; what was this? I didn't know who these women were or how I was supposed to help them.

And just as I started to sink, I thought of Nan and I tried praying. I was in such a frenzy that I could not think of anything except, "Lord Jesus Help." As soon as the words left my lips, I heard that friendly, small voice whispering to me.

"I am with you." I knew then what I was supposed to do.

I began to command the waves to cease, and the water began to recede, and the women were cheering and I looked up and stretched my hands to the sky. I think I was about to say *thank you*, but just like that it was over and I was back in my bed fast asleep.

My cell phone alarm buzzed and violently yanked me out of my dream. I sat up with hair all over the place, eyes closed and my arms were reaching towards the ceiling. I was covered in sweat, and I had the worst headache. I felt for my phone on the nightstand but I wasn't ready to open my eyes. I fumbled in the dark trying to turn it off, and then

I lay there for a while. I needed to calm my thoughts. I think I was still in shock from the dream.

After I steadied my breathing, I slowly opened my eyes, but I didn't move for a while. I sat there in bed staring straight ahead trying to process that dream. How could a dream seem so real? I really felt like all of it was real.

Was God telling me something? Was I supposed to save someone or maybe I was supposed to save myself. God was chasing me; I was his beloved but I was out here looking for my beloved. It still hadn't occurred to me that I was a part of the greatest love story that had ever been told. *If you are looking for love, has it ever occurred to you that God loves you and is ready and willing to fill you up with his love? Perhaps that is the love you are seeking and you just don't know it yet.*

The temperature in the room felt normal again and after about twenty minutes, I was ready to get out of bed, but not before I checked the floor to make sure there were no rising waters or hidden oceans. Once I was convinced the coast was clear, I started laughing at myself, and then I allowed my feet to touch the floor.

I went through my normal routine of getting ready for the day and once again I pushed the experience to the back of my mind. I wanted to stay busy allowing myself no real time to sit still and figure it all out. I quickly showered and put my hair into a bun. I threw on black tights, my black boots, and my grey stained sweatshirt. This sweatshirt was dear to me, one day I threw it in the wash with a few other things forgetting to check the pockets of my pants and it came out beautifully ruined in the silhouette of *Nina Simone* or at least I think so. It was a no make-up kind of day because I was only meeting Daniel. I was dressed and ready to go.

I walked to the kitchen and smelled the dark roast coffee. Kristen and Gary were into their morning papers. I peeked in to say *Good Morning* and grab my oversized black scarf from the counter. I received a half-hearted good morning from both of them so I decided to get coffee on the way to class once I met Daniel. I hit the streets and as usual the city was alive; I was just about to call Daniel to find out if we had time to stop for coffee, but I felt like I was being watched.

I looked around and everything seemed normal, but I could have sworn I saw Gerald's black Mercedes turn the corner. I was probably seeing things. I could only imagine how many people owned that type of black Mercedes in this part of New York. After a few seconds I shook off the creeps and dialed Daniel; he picked up on the first ring making me smile.

"Hello Good Looking. Are you all ready to embarrass yourself?"

I guess an impromptu class could be embarrassing, but for some reason knowing that Daniel would be there put me at ease.

"Yup all ready to make a fool out of myself. So where should we meet?"

He said the class was in Midtown which was about twenty minutes from the Ansonia.

I purposely didn't ask Kristen for the car service. I was still up in the air about how long I would stay in New York, and before I left I was going to become a pro at hailing cabs.

It was 8:30 am, and I felt powerful as I stood at the far end of the corner of the building as the doorman Carl eyed me strangely. He must have thought I was nuts when I clearly could have used the car service. I was far enough away to be seen but no so far that I could get run down by a crazed yellow cab.

After about ten minutes, I was in the back of a lemon-scented cab; the driver played soothing Middle Eastern music. I gave him the address; he smiled kindly and I was off to meet Daniel. He sipped on his coffee and boy did it smell lovely. I watched him intently as he took sip after sip; I was actually tempted to ask for some. I had forgotten to ask Daniel if there were any good coffee places around class. I'm sure there were at least ten coffee places near the class, but I was a coffee aficionado and only coffee aficionados would understand the difference between good coffee and great coffee.

The cab ride was calming; he stopped at every light and he drove like a normal person. I was pleasantly surprised. He slowed down and smiled and said my total was $25. I expected it to be more, so I gave him $35 and thanked him for a safe drive. He smiled and nodded. Wow he was gorgeous! He wore a modest wedding band and I wondered if his wife was gorgeous, too. My thoughts of the beautiful Middle Eastern stranger were interrupted when Daniel opened my car door and handed me a steaming hot cup of coffee. I was on my second pleasant surprise of the day and it wasn't even noon yet.

Daniel really was thoughtful. "I thought you might want another cup; I'm sure you already had one with your sister."

He watched me as I sipped and let the coffee travel down before I answered him. I was enjoying this moment. He laughed at me.

"This is actually my first cup and you don't know how much this means to me."

He waved me off and laughed again. After a few more sips we walked arm in arm into the building. This place smelled like sweat and everyone was dressed like they were at the gym. I guess we fit right in minus the sweat. Daniel and I were almost identically dressed—black bottoms and grey tops.

These actors looked serious and I felt a little intimidated. We were in a plain, medium-sized room, nothing too special, but I could tell everyone in this place had something special. I could see the hunger I their eyes and I hoped that I would be good today. An older slightly grey haired slender brunette of medium height read our names from a clip board. Her voice was stern and hints of beauty were etched in her weathered face. I imagined her as a late 1950 something pinup girl turning heads and breaking hearts.

She called our names and we were instructed to take off our shoes. Ok this was going to be interesting. She turned off all the lights except for one, a small spotlight in the middle of the room. She stepped into the spotlight and began to speak.

"Many of you think you know me, but you do not know me at all."

She said she had been in television and film for over twenty years. There were many confused looks in the room because this woman was not recognizable to any of us. She said that many actors want to be on the A-list and they get discouraged if they never reach that pinnacle of success, but the blue collar actors get supporting roles in many large productions and are always working. Ok this made sense.

She stepped out of the spotlight and pushed a shocked young guy into her place; she hissed like a snake and walked around him slowly as if he were prey.

"Hello Henry, where the Hell is my money?" she asked.

This woman's portrayal of a snake was so incredible. I thought she was going to bite poor Henry and apparently so did poor Henry; he didn't understand the definition of impromptu because he just stood there frozen. She kept hissing at him, and then it hit me, *oh crap class had begun.* Without warning my very first impromptu class had started. I was so excited, my fingers were prickly and I had a huge lump in my throat. Daniel whispered to me to breathe, but before I could, he left my side and stepped in the spotlight and transformed into a baboon, dragging his arms as if they weighed a ton.

In a loud voice he yelled, "Back away from the kid. I have the money."

I was amazed. How did he know how to participate? I guessed I really should have taken his class back in Philly. She hissed and he beat his chest like a wild baboon; they circled one another looking for the money and poor Henry was paralyzed. I felt like I was watching an episode of *Animal Planet* on *Discovery.* Henry looked green, but I thought better him than me. The rest of us watched the instructor and her new favorite student.

I was ready to get in there but another person stepped in and purred like a cat. This mystery woman was a little too close to Daniel's face; I thought they might kiss and for some strange reason, this made me jealous and of course it didn't help that she was a beautiful red-haired Ginger.

"I don't have the money, but I think I know who does," she said.

She spoke slowly rocking her hips around Daniel and purring like a jungle cat.

"Let me help you get the money".

She wrapped her legs around his and leaned so far back I thought she was going to fall but of course Daniel held her up. And there they were entangled in some sort of wild kingdom mix; her long red hair spilled out of Daniels hands and I was pissed. I didn't even think about how I would get in; I just went for it. I started wildly flapping my arms like an angry bird, but I never moved into the spotlight and then out of nowhere I screamed, "*CACAWL, CACAWL.*"

The entire class froze and looked at me. Daniel smiled. I think he felt embarrassed for me, and I silently prayed to disappear. The instructor turned the lights back on and announced that the exercise was over. Oh, gosh I wanted to die. I tried my best to act natural. Ginger smirked and giggled, but some people patted me on the back. Did I pass or fail? I was so confused.

The instructor took her seat and we all followed her lead. I noticed Daniel sat next to Ginger and something burned in my chest. What was this about? Daniel and I were just friends and I made a mental note to prove it. The instructor stood up and the class began to stand, but she waved for us to stay seated. Her eyes searched the students, and I felt uneasy, partially because I didn't have Daniel sitting next to me and partially because I didn't know what would come next.

Then all of a sudden, she threw her chair in the middle of the floor, we all jumped and poor Henry grabbed his coat and ran out. She didn't even flinch and then she spoke, "Quick thinking, digging deep and chutzpa make an actor".

She burned with passion; she said at times you will be required to fill in the gaps of a script." Her fists were raised to the ceiling as she said, "Will you run out or will you rise to the challenge?" I let her question sink in for a moment; was I actually ready to rise to the challenge?

This class was terrifying. She said you must learn to trust yourself. For some reason the thought of trusting myself moved me to tears, but I couldn't have an *emo* moment when I was too busy watching Ginger coo and giggle at Daniel.

We were asked to pair off in groups of three and she gave us scenarios but no instructions and by the third exercise I was a big ball of energy. One part of me wanted to run out like poor Henry but another part of me burned with a conceivable truth from within and I knew I had to stay. I'm not sure if my choices were correct, but I never followed poor Henry out that door and for that I was proud.

The Class ended with everyone introducing themselves and sharing stories about acting experiences in New York. When it was my turn, I stood up, my palms were sweaty and in an uncertain voice I said, "Hello I'm Athena, this is my second class here in New York and I've been on one audition." There was a weird pause and I could here whispers around the room and I knew some of the students were in shock, the instructor just smiled and ginger looked annoyed.

Daniel also smiled as I talked about how I ran out of the theatre and made some guy chase me, although I never used his name we both knew the guy was him. As I was talking he moved closer to me and then he held my hand. I resisted the urge to stick my tongue out at Ginger as if I were an elementary school child. The instructor told me that took guts to go on an audition with no training and I should keep going. I nervously took her advice and said my good-byes to the other students; the class was four hours long and I was starving.

I waited outside for Daniel, still covered in nervous sweat. The chill quickly dried my sweatshirt and the wet hairs on the back of my neck. I leaned against the wall with my eyes closed and I could feel the peace in the moment. I didn't know how I knew but I knew it was God. My quiet moment was interrupted from all of my missed calls from Carmen, my phone wouldn't stop ringing, so I finally picked up, I was so excited and I wanted to tell her everything.

"Hey Carm." It was good to hear her voice.

"Hey sister, Mary and I thought it would be a good idea for us to come up Saturday".

I didn't want to share this trip with my girls, so I changed the subject and told her all about the two classes I took, bumping into Daniel and meeting Gerald.

"Hmm do we have a few mystery lovers?" she said in a phony British accent, Carm really was nuts.

I decided to leave out the dream and the closet experience. I explained that I had been so busy I may not have time for the night life. I felt like I should have told her what was really going on with me, but I was afraid to let that part of me go. ***How many of us have people we can be free with?*** I knew she would have allowed me to be myself but I just couldn't do it. So I pretended like most of us do and told her everything was fine. She said Mary was working on a new blog post and would call me later. My line beeped and there was that familiar electricity. I could no longer concentrate on my conversation with Carm. I watched his number flash and my insides were weak. I got a quick image of a disapproving Nan shaking her head at me but I shook it off. I quickly hung up with Carmen and started fixing myself. I wanted to look my best, but why was I fixing myself as if he could see me?

"Hello Gerald," I said.

Ginger and Daniel were coming out of the door and the look on my face stopped Daniel in his tracks. I could see him watching and he looked tense but I couldn't deal with Daniel and his tense face.

"Hello Pretty Lady, are you busy?"

I told Gerald I was just leaving class. "Where are you? I'll come get you," he said.

I was kind of getting use to his demands.

"I really can't, I had class and lunch plans, remember?"

After Daniel's failed attempt at eavesdropping, he slowly inched away from Ginger and was basically standing over me. I asked Gerald to hold on and I took the phone away from my ear. "Can I help you, sir?" I asked.

Daniel's posture became hard at the sound of Gerald's name.

I think that Ginger got the point because she sucked her teeth and said, "Um, Hello."

Daniel asked her to give him a second, but she crossed her arms over her chest and walked away. I gestured for him to go after her but he never moved. I felt uncomfortable with his standing there, so I rushed Gerald off the phone. I could feel the heat through the phone as I said goodbye; Gerald was upset. Daniel started that clenched-jaw thing I've seen men do before. This was always an indicator that something was wrong.

"Good class, huh," he said.

Ok, he wanted to play it cool as if he wasn't about to blow. "Yeah, great class. Where did Ginger--oops, I mean what's her name—-go?"

He started cracking up and this eased the tension between us. I had to find out why he had such an issue with Gerald and today had to be the day. I was starving but dismissed his idea for Chinese. I wanted an authentic New York vendor hot dog and Daniel insisted that I let him grab the cab this time. I could tell Daniel had something to ask me, but I kept him on the subject of class; I didn't want to get heavy until after we ate.

I was a little jealous because his cab-hailing skills were excellent; we pulled up to a vendor on Fifth Avenue and East 62nd Street near the Central Park Zoo and I could smell the hot dogs in the air. I was so excited I rushed out of the car and left Daniel. The line was long and the crowd was all over the place. I happily took my place in a line of ten people and my insides giggled as I got closer. Daniel finally joined me.

"Wow! I have never seen a person so excited about a hot dog," he said.

I people-watched and listened to the chatter. Some children were laughing and some were throwing tantrums. Perfectly manicured mommies and nannies scheduled play dates on their smart phones.

Everything was perfect and then he did it. I really wasn't ready for it at all. He turned to me with deep concern in his eyes and I remembered that I'd seen that look before on Kristen's face. We were moving closer to the front of the line, and he blurted out: "Athena, Gerald Gleason is not a person that you should connect with."

And just like that the happy moment was over and the atmosphere was different. What did he mean by this? Was I not good enough to be connected to a wealthy, powerful man that actually seemed to like me? It's funny how I took Daniel's words and heard only what I wanted to hear because I wanted to do only what I wanted to do. I asked him to hold that thought and I turned to the smiling, plump-faced man standing before me.

"What will it be sweetheart?" he asked.

Daniel was not letting up. He was stern and making sure I understood what he was saying; he turned me back to face him.

"This is not a game. I haven't known you forever but we aren't strangers either." He said he knew enough to know that Gerald was not for me. And again the plump-faced man asked--but this time with annoyance--"What will it be sweetheart?"

I pulled away from Daniel and ordered two hot dogs with raw onions, extra sauerkraut, mustard and a ginger-ale soda. Man the smell of this food had me high. I basically swallowed one of the hot dogs before we could find a bench to sit and talk. I wasn't sure if it was because I ate the hot dogs so fast or because I knew I had to respond to Daniel, but I felt sick and a little off. The air was thick and the mood was fickle; I wasn't sure if this would end with Daniel's yelling or my defending my right to date Gerald.

"Listen. I thank you for your concern but what is so bad about my hanging with one of New York's finest?"

"Tuh, Huh," he winced at my comment, and then he cursed under his breath and spit his hot dog out on the ground.

Daniel had mustard on the corner of his mouth and he was angry. He told me that Gerald Gleason was an old business partner and ex friend of his family's and they were connected through New York social circles. Gerald was caught in a big scandal which resulted in a divorce and his ex-wife's making claims of physical and verbal abuse. It was also rumored that he had heavy ties to criminal business deals and sadistic sex clubs, and he would shut anyone down that told him *no*.

Ok, I could see the not-taking-no-for-an-answer part because you have to be tough to reach the level of success that he had. The sex club seemed like a reach because Gerald seemed too refined for that. I had a lump in my throat the size of North Dakota because I remembered his friend's private club he tried to take me to. I wondered if he was actually trying to take me to *that* kind of place. I'd just had a bomb dropped on me. So I sat there and tried to focus on the park bench. I forced my mind to travel to how many stories were told in this very spot.

I couldn't find the words to respond. I kept hearing the word *alleged* in my mind. Were these just rumors? Was Daniel truly concerned or was he jealous like I had been a few hours ago about him and Ginger? I finally turned to him; he looked like he was preparing for a storm.

"Daniel, thank you so much for your concern, but I'm a big girl. I will do some investigations on my own."

My response infuriated him but before he could respond, I leaned in, kissed him on the cheek and walked off. I could hear him behind me cursing and asking what he had to do to get through to me, but I never turned around.

Dancing with the Devil

I had to clear my mind and speak with Gerald to settle this matter quickly. I walked out of Central Park and hailed a cab, and apparently I was as good as Daniel because I got one to stop with ease. For some reason I felt like Daniel would come chasing after me and deep down inside I think I wanted him to; man did I have issues. So far there was no sign of Daniel. I even started slowly walking towards the cab to give him an opportunity to catch me before I got in.

I was angry but who was I angry with? I needed to prove Daniel was wrong about Gerald. Something was nagging at my heart and I knew I should go back and find him, but I also knew I wanted him to be wrong which made me even angrier. This could possibly be my chance to have a successful man and I was not in the mood to hear, "Oh P.S. he may be a psychopath."

And as far as we gals go, some of us are still secretly on a quest to become *Mrs. Such-and-Such or So-and-So* and run from who we are called to be. ***Could it be that it is easier to attach ourselves to his dreams instead of going after our own?***

I got in the back of the cab and headed to Kristen's when my phone rang. The butterflies leaped in my stomach; I knew it was Daniel calling to ask me to come back. I decided to make him sweat for upsetting me. I would make him ask twice and then I would have the cab driver turn around and go back. I giggled to myself, and the cab driver watched me curiously in his mirror.

"Penny for your thoughts," he said.

I never got to answer the driver. I looked at my phone and it was Gerald. I watched the *212* flash on my screen; I had gotten used to preparing myself before I answered his calls, and I guessed this was as good a time as any to settle the matter of his character.

"Hi Gerald; we need to talk; I have a few questions to ask you." My voice was set in that matter-of-fact tone and I had my brave face on. Before he answered he started laughing, which made me uncomfortable, and I started to squirm in my seat. What was so funny? I guessed he didn't know that the joke would be on him if I did not like his answers.

"Ok Doll Face this sounds serious. When and where?"

Of course I let him pick the place because I didn't have many places in New York. But I did manage to put my foot down and suggest having coffee. I wasn't in the mood for fancy bottles of wine that cost more than a month's rent; no upscale, intimate chef specials and no designer shoes that pinched my toes. The ride back to Kristen's was a little somber. I kept replaying the conversation with Daniel in my mind and practicing the conversation I would have with Gerald, which terrified me, but I had to get it over with.

I arrived back at the Ansonia and quickly showered off the class sweat and stepped into the closet with a little bit of uneasiness. I don't think I'll ever look at a closet the same again. I threw on a casual burgundy skirt and t-shirt and paired it with my motorcycle bomber; this jacket always made me feel empowered. I quietly rushed to the door and purposely avoided Kristen and Gary.

Gerald said he'd be in the lobby in 45 minutes and judging by the last time we met, that meant 30 minutes.

I got close to the door and Kristen yell, "Well hello to you too." *Oh crap! I was caught!*

I walked back into the living room to see her in some weird twisted yoga pose with Gary doing a downward dog—these two were perfect for each other. "I'm sorry; I have coffee with Gerald," I said.

She looked confused. "I thought you had class with Daniel?"

I avoided her gaze and headed out the door. "I'll see you later." The elevator ride felt full of live wires tingling all over me and for some reason I thought of Nan. I felt she wanted me to go back upstairs, but I kept riding further and further until I was in the lobby. The doors slowly opened and Daniel was standing there; I jumped back; I wasn't expecting him, but a big part of me was happy to see him. He grabbed my elbows and pulled me close. His breath smelled like hotdogs and I liked it. I thought he might kiss me. What was I doing?

"Hey, I know it's weird for me to just show up, but I had to apologize about the park."

I was silent and my mouth was wide open. I couldn't believe that he was apologizing to me after I stormed off. I had tears in my eyes and I rushed to hug him; the moment was so special I almost forgot about Gerald. I forced myself out of our embrace and explained that I was meeting Gerald at this second to discuss the new turn of events.

The look on Daniel's face broke my heart, but he kissed me on the cheek and lowered his head and mouthed a somber, "Call you later."

Draped in confusion, I walked past Daniel toward the front doors. Nan would always say that, "God is not the God of confusion but the God of Peace, and right now I really needed to slow down and get some peace."

Gerald's alluring magic still appealed to me and I managed to convince myself that I needed to find out about his past. I walked toward that front door; Gerald was waiting for me. He was leaning against a military style black Mercedes Benz SUV.

He had on a black suit and aviator shades; he looked like a general. I walked over to him and he extended his hand to take mine, and then he kissed it gently and again there was that voodoo. I climbed in the truck but I said nothing. I felt nervous and I swore to myself that I would stay in control. This time he sat far away, but his eyes said it all; he wouldn't stop staring and I couldn't stop thinking.

What if Daniel was right? What if my connection to Gerald would take me down a path I couldn't come back from? As we drove to the coffee shop I wondered where I was allowing myself to be led. I contemplated having his driver stop the truck; I'd get out and let it be.

"Hey there beautiful, you look like you are in deep thought."

I smiled at him and explained that I had been thinking about auditions. The SUV pulled up to a luxurious coffee spot called "*Delicieux.*" This place was a Parisian paradise fit for Josephine Baker or Queen Catherine de' Medici of France.

Gerald was well known by the staff, and the manager personally came out to greet us. He lightly clapped his bony fingers as he complimented Gerald on his suit. This guy must have earned a master's degree in suck-up because he kept going on and on. I walked away from them to get a quiet moment alone and to observe the place.

Wow, I got a little taste of France in a bakery/coffee shop on Madison Avenue. The color of the pastries danced from behind the pristine glass casing; the soft pastels made my mouth water. The chairs reminded me of Gerald's chairs at *Peixe.* The craftsmanship was so mesmerizing that I started to imagine myself as a Lady in a French Court. Small messages were written in French on the napkins. I picked one up and tried to sound it out *V-e-n-i-r.*

Gerald came behind me and started reading with ease, translating for me, "*Venir en France et de vous retrouver,*" which means come to France and find yourself. I wasn't shocked that he could speak fluent French; he was cultured and well versed in the art of everything.

This Parisian bakery almost became a distraction, and although I enjoyed my French lesson, there was a point to our meeting, so I sat down and prepared to order. I chose a molasses flavored brew and a *Tarte Tatin.* I needed to sip this coffee before I got to my questions. It was the strongest coffee I had ever tasted and the bold flavors danced on my tongue. I took one more sip and now I was ready to begin.

I sat up straight so I would look serious. "Gerald, I wanted to talk with you because I heard some not-so-good things about your past and I want to clear the air."

He blinked. He appeared unnerved. "There's an old saying that my mother use to say, "Beware of the messenger," he said.

I thought of Daniel; did I really need to beware of Daniel? This was all so confusing. Gerald sat up straight and cleared his throat.

"Ok, shoot. For you, my dear, I'm an open book."

I started with questions on his ex-wife and the abuse and I saved the criminal activity for last. I was too shy to discuss the sex clubs, but if there was even a hint of guilt I would assume that everything was true and that would be enough for me. He took a sip of his latte before he answered. He looked hurt but he was holding something back. He reached across the table and grabbed my hand. Oh my, he actually had tears in his eyes! Either he was the biggest liar or I was the biggest jerk for bringing up something that was obviously painful for him. In a subdued tone he said that his ex-wife wanted a divorce because he travelled a lot for business; the divorce turned nasty and one night they got into a heated argument.

"She got drunk and attacked me because she thought I was seeing another woman," he said.

He seemed so sincere.

"I may have grabbed her arm a little too hard but just to calm her, and the next thing I knew she was asking for half of everything or she was going to the police with abuse charges."

I wondered how hard was *too hard*. He held my hands tight. He was shaking when he said he had something to tell me. I braced myself.

"One of my divorce attorneys was Daniel's father."

Ok, the cat was out of the bag. I searched his face for a reaction, and then he sternly said, "You know Athena some people are not what they seem."

Was Daniel not what he seemed? What was going on? I really needed Nan right now; she always knew what to do and I knew she'd tell me to pray. So why wasn't I praying because I really needed answers. Gerald never said anything about the information, but I knew that he knew it came from Daniel. He said the case never went anywhere and he was never formally charged. He eventually divorced her; she didn't get the money she pushed for and as promised she did slander his name amongst New York's most elite circles.

"Athena I worked hard to clean up my reputation, and I'm proud of the work I've accomplished."

I was silent for a while because I was confused. A part of me felt ashamed for asking and another part of me wanted to question him further. I was angry with Daniel for putting me in this situation and still angry with myself because I felt there was some truth to Daniel's story. I apologized for prying; we finished our French treats and talked some more before heading back to the SUV. From that moment on I never questioned his character although there were many occasions when I should have. I requested he drop me off a few blocks from the Ansonia. I wanted to walk and get lost in my thoughts. We said our good-byes and made plans for Saturday night, but I wasn't sure if I would keep them. I thought it was time to pray.

A Little Bit of R & R

The walk back to the Ansonia was full of questions, so I began asking them. "Hi God I know we haven't seriously talked since the closet, but I need help. Ummm, so there's this guy."

Ok, I was not about to have the so-there's-this-guy conversation with God, so I stopped myself and got real.

"God, something's missing inside. I feel that it may consume me if I don't find it; please help me." And as quickly as the last words fell from my lips, a calm came over my body and I knew I wasn't alone and I also knew what I needed to do. I ignored all of Gerald's calls and texts for the next couple of weeks, but I managed to text Daniel to let him know I needed space. Gerald didn't like the distance between us; he tried whatever he could to get my attention. The concierge's desk at the Ansonia was constantly full of roses, orchids and lilies; I had my very own personal flower show. I gave some of the flowers to the female staff members. Gerald's antics were starting to annoy Kristen and Gary, but they left the damage control to me and the only thing I knew to do was to ignore him.

I went on two auditions. One was for a reality show which I didn't want to do, but I heard that reality stars were getting sitcom offers and some were going on to do Broadway productions, so I gave it a try. The other audition was for an up-and-coming hair care company called, *Paradise on Earth Organics.* I knew there wasn't much acting involved but it was still a job. I thought I might get this one because the director was in love with my mane; he shrieked when I walked in and without my permission ran his fingers through it. I was proud of myself for fighting for my reason to come to New York. And even though it felt like an uphill battle, at least I had let go of the little mouse that thought she could never audition.

I was still confused and not ready to talk to Daniel. Growing up I would always hear Nan tell Teresa that it was not good to address a person that you cared about when you were confused and I did care for Daniel. Nan said it was better to ask God to deal with it, so I did. And I still had that sticky feeling somewhere deep inside because I didn't trust Gerald. The thought of calling him caused a lump in my throat because I may have swallowed a lie. ***Does this sound familiar to anyone? The lies we accept are like fading lamp posts miles away from the shore of truth that could set us free.*** And secretly all I wanted was to be set free. I wanted to be set free from the fear that I would never become a Broadway actress, I wanted to be free of wanting someone and I wanted to be free of feeling that I wasn't enough. I was so chained in bondage that I never stopped to see what was in front of my face.

All of this trying-to-keep-it-together nonsense was starting to give me a headache, so I decided to tour some museums. I finally made up my mind and went to the Museum of Modern Art. I did an online search and since I was looking for a distraction from dealing with my mess, the cinema exhibits appealed to me. I threw on my burnt orange knee-length sweater dress and my old pork pie hat that had belonged to pop. I let my hair hang wild today. I thought I should look a little artsy considering I was going to a museum. I avoided Kristen and Gary; I wasn't in the mood to talk to them or bear witness to their happy laughter and I knew Kristen would see right through me.

I decided to catch the subway so I could people watch again. I knew that would take my mind off me. I got a little confused with the metro cards, but after a few tries, I figured it out. I found out the hard way that I had to take the #6 train to get there, but I almost missed the E train because I didn't know I had to transfer. Sheesh the New York transit system confused me. After an extra fifteen minutes I had finally arrived. I walked up the dirty staircase that smelled of rotten pizza and urine. I spent a moment adjusting my bearings and found the Museum of Modern Art. I walked in and my heart skipped a beat when I saw the theatre and cinema exhibits.

I studied the black and white photographs and I tried to recognize the nameless faces on the life-changing stages. I imagined them demanding to be seen during a time when no one wanted to see their kind. I wondered if they knew they paved the way for a girl like me to have a chance to be one of the greats. ***How does anyone gain the courage to go after their dreams?*** I heard someone say somewhere, "Never despise small beginnings," and to "Trust the process." Well this was me and here I was in the beginning and trying my best to trust in my small processes. And of course I got emotional staring at the exhibits and the tears started to flow. The air was clean and everyone was into their own experience, so I didn't think anyone noticed my mini meltdown until I heard the jingle of keys behind me. I turned and there stood a small man in a security guard uniform.

"Whoever he is, he's not worth it." Ok, so someone had noticed my dramatic display of emotions. I smiled, wiped my face and quickly walked away. There was something about his words that touched my heart and made me think of Officer Kendrick. I wondered what he was doing; maybe I would mystery dial him later just to hear that soothing voice. There was something so warm about him. I walked around the theatre and took in a few more exhibits; each time I imagined myself in the scene; I wanted success so bad. I noticed a cool exhibit dedicated to peace and it had nothing to do with theatre or cinema, but I decided to check it out. The crowd in front of a painting was large but silent because the flowing river commanded a presence and so we all stopped and stared. After a while the artist proudly stood by it and described his inspiration.

This guy's audience was large and mainly female and I could see why; he was beautiful in a Disney Prince Charming kind of way. I stood off to the side and listened to him talk about what peace meant to him and what this painting represented.

His voice was tranquil, "Peace is like a silent inner river that continually flows and no matter the situation good or bad, you're always confident that it will work out." I laughed out loud because it sounded like he was quoting

Nan; this was how Nan talked about having Christ; this guy had to have known her. I guess I laughed too loud because everyone including Prince Charming turned to watch me. I was embarrassed and I quickly apologized, coughed a little and pretended something was stuck in my throat. After a few angry art fans agreed to accept my apology, everyone turned back to Charming. His words were honest and pure like the Chicken-Soup-for-the-Soul guy. He spoke of peace as if it were a part of his DNA. I really wanted to know this peace he painted. I hung around the exhibit until the end to get a closer look at his peace not knowing I actually did have my own and if I would be willing then the true author of peace would show me how to get it. This river he painted flowed in 3D; I wanted to reach out and touch it. I could feel his presence behind me; I could also smell his scent; he smelled like oil paint, fresh mints and oak; it was an odd mixture that made a pleasant mash of who he probably was.

He was polite as he introduced himself, "Hello I'm Wyatt Bretwater." My gosh, his smile melted my heart; his hair was a muddy dark brown; he towered over me like an athlete. *Wow an athletic painter* I said to myself.

"I'm not very athletic," he said. I was blushing.

"I thought I said that in my head." We both laughed.

His face had a translucent glow and his brown eyes looked right through me. Oh man was I in trouble. He explained that this was his first showing in a major museum and a few short years ago he was a starving artist from Wyoming.

"Well Wyatt Bretwater from Wyoming, this is my first time in New York and it has been eventful." I turned back to his painting to take it all in. I needed peace so I stood and watched the river flow and imagined the sounds of an enchanted forest. I introduced myself and to my surprise I asked him out for coffee and tea. I wasn't sure of his preference. I had enough coffee in my body to last another two days, but I wanted to stay close to Wyatt and his peace and that was the only thing I could think of. I desperately needed to get lost in his story for a little while; I got so excited when he agreed.

We walked a few blocks from the museum to an outdated café with dull floors and tattered chairs. This place was ten steps down from the French café I visited with Gerald, but Wyatt's temperament was so calming I was hardly bothered. He said this place was special because it was the first place he noticed, before walking into the museum and changing his life. I let those words linger in my head; he changed his life in one moment; would I ever become fearless enough to take my moment? This place was owned by a beautiful Jamaican family that served a piece of the islands in every cup. Wyatt and I sat on one of the old tattered chairs and talked about life.

"You seemed troubled," he said. I wondered what vibe I was giving off. I tried my best to leave the drama behind and focus on today. I don't know why I told a complete stranger about my dating woes but out came the story of Gerald, Daniel and Broadway. He listened intently as I discussed my experiences with the guys and auditioning. He flashed that smile again and I let out a sigh.

"It's kind of like we are all out here searching for something we lost at the beginning of time." His words choked me up a little because that was exactly how I felt. I wondered how many people were walking around chasing their destinies and trying to find some sort of missing birthright. Were we all desperately trying to get back to who we truly are?

One of the owner's daughters, Fiona, invited me to try some homemade gingerbread. She looked as if she had been dipped in a bucket of bronze paint; her gold bangles shined in all of their glory and her dark hair hung off her shoulders; she was really beautiful. I felt as if I were meeting the real life Cleopatra. She was slender but at the same time voluptuous and earthy. Fiona seemed to be the kind of woman that was wise beyond her years but free as a child. She handed me a slice of gingerbread and spiced tea.

"Here, to calm your nerves," she whispered and winked at me.

I guessed everyone could see my distress. Wyatt and I talked until the placed closed and this was exactly what I needed. He told me that it was okay to pray, that he did it all the time and without it he felt lost. He kissed me on the hand; we exchanged numbers and we stood to go our separate ways. I walked out of *Jamba Jemma's* feeling full and not from the bread; I stole some of Wyatt's peace or maybe I finally tapped into my own.

I floated down the street engrossed in my thoughts. I wondered why I had sworn off men and yet I was some kind of man magnet. What was the purpose of my bumping into Daniel after all this time, going out with Gerald and now Wyatt from Wyoming? And why was I still thinking of Officer Kendrick? I could now find the humor in how we try to settle things on our own without help as if we are the ones that are really in control. I walked the streets until I got lost trying to figure it all out even though that was the last thing I wanted to do and I had forgotten all about Wyatt's advice to pray. I reached for my phone to check in with Kristen and noticed I had many missed calls. One from Kristen, two from Daniel and fifteen from Gerald.

I headed toward the subway and I called Gerald back first because I knew something was wrong. "Hello Gerald is everything ok?" I could hear him breathing, but he stayed silent for a few seconds.

"Where are you?" he asked and he seemed upset. I told him about clearing my head and auditioning without distraction.

"Oh, sorry that our friendship is a distraction."

I guess he noticed that I was purposely avoiding him, but his reaction was not normal, and he was way too intense. His attitude annoyed me, but I was in such peace from talking with Wyatt that I apologized to calm him.

"Don't you ever!" he yelled, then paused quickly, took a breath and calmed himself. "I'm sorry baby but after our

last talk I was worried that you wanted to stop our friendship."

Now I was the one pausing to collect myself. I thought we needed to take a break from the intensity; this internal pushing towards him was wearing me out. I had come to New York to audition and not to date and I didn't know why I was still trying to reason with myself. I knew what the correct choice was.

"Look Gerald. I need time to clear my head and audition. I will call you later." Before he could speak, my phone disconnected. I was underground in the train station. Saved by the lack of cell service! Whew!

I waited for the train and took a deep breath of whatever the yuck, was that lingered in the air and watched the tiny person in pigtails trying to let go of her mother's hand. ***Why can't we all approach life the way children do?*** They are always ready to run free and let go. My phone started ringing and this time I decided to stand up to Gerald and tell him I needed space permanently. "Hello Athena speaking," I said.

"Hello this is Wyatt Bretwater." I was so relieved and now I was curious as to why Wyatt would call so soon.

"Well usually I'm not so forward, but I really enjoyed our conversation; would you like to have dinner?"

He explained that he had a plus one to an art mixer and dinner and he hated going to those things alone. He didn't demand that I get all dolled up. He didn't even give me the time speech. The mixer was in 30 minutes, so I gave myself a few quick sprays of *Lady Bug*, ran my fingers through my hair, adjusted my pork pie and reapplied my lip gloss. I decided to get off the train at the next stop and try out the new car app that Kristen finally downloaded to my phone. I didn't have time to hail a cab. Ok so if I could remember from her technical babbling that I had to sign into this thing. But first I had to get outside. My phone service was back to being janky down here.

I was nervous to be in the car with a stranger, but I guess it was the same as the yellow cab so I waited on the corner of West 25th Street; the car pulled up and looked like a stunt car from that movie *Tokyo Drift*. I laughed at being seen in this bright green racer, but I climbed in anyway and was off to a place called *"Rouge."* I felt a strange energy before I got out and I knew tonight I would replace one distraction with another. Rouge was crowded but not uncomfortable. I watched Wyatt as he sat in the window, and I pushed the strange energy out of my mind. I tapped on the window to let him know I had arrived. I must have startled him because he dropped his phone and a tipsy woman in an oversized pump almost destroyed it.

"I'm sorry," I said and gave him my best apologetic eyes. After Wyatt rescued his phone, he turned back toward the window and smiled at me; hmmm there was no hidden agenda behind his smile. He pointed to the front door and wiggled through the crowd to come and get me. We eventually found a quiet spot in the back of the madness we ordered shrimp spring rolls and red wine. The spring rolls took my mind off of my madness.

"Hey thanks for coming on such short notice," he said. I was so excited to be here with genuine artists. He said he wanted to know more about my art and anything that I wanted to tell him. I was stuck on this question because I was no artist. Back in high school I could sketch a mean Mickey Mouse, but it was nothing compared to what Wyatt could do.

"Athena, we all have hidden art, buried deep inside our souls and until we provoke it, the art lies quiet, waiting for its chance to be used."

All I could muster up to reply to that statement was a "Wow." He smiled tenderly and said, "I think you are already your own walking Picasso."

Wyatt was deep and gorgeous. I couldn't handle his sensitivity so I changed the subject quickly before I started getting emotional, and I asked him about his next piece. He said it was called Grace. He explained how he would try his best to convey Grace through his art and it gave me chills. I wanted to kiss him but instead I started tearing up. I excused myself and quickly tried to walk away but he grabbed me, turned my face toward his and wiped my tears. He kissed me on my forehead, and then he kissed the bridge of my nose, and then he went back to my forehead; my breathing intensified. I placed my hand on his chest; I could feel his heart jumping around. He sat there inches from my lips as if he were waiting for permission, so I moved closer and I gave it to him. We were kissing and panting and kissing and panting; this attraction felt more than physical. I was confused, but I couldn't stop myself. What was I doing? The last thing I needed was a full make out session in public with a new guy. ***Why do we continue to do the things that we say we will never do again?***

Wyatt wasn't grabby or disrespectful; he was gentle as he pulled me in for more. "What's happening here?" I whispered. He shushed me and kissed me hard. This kiss felt nothing like Gerald's kiss. I wanted this and I wanted him. I knew this was wrong; I had to stop this.

The server cleared his throat and interrupted us; we finally took a break for air and noticed that we were being photographed. Lights were flashing from every direction and people were watching us; some smiled, some applauded and I think a few ladies were jealous.

Wyatt looked green as the flashing continued and I noticed a hint of guilt or embarrassment on his face. Oh no, I knew this look all too well and I felt as if I had been punched. "Sorry that we were photographed and now I'm guessing you're in trouble, right?"

I had to get out of there; I wanted to run off and leave him to deal with the crowd. I snatched my purse and knocked the last of my red wine all over the table. The server frantically dashed to clean up the mess.

Wyatt still had that stupid look on his face and I was hot inside, drunk, and my feelings were hurt. Oh, Athena why do you get yourself in these situations? He chased after me and grabbed my arm. I snatched it away and tried not to make a scene as I stumbled and wobbled to keep my balance. "What in the heck is wrong with you and why would I be in trouble?" He said.

I started screaming, "I know that look, you peaceful jerk, you have a girlfriend!" Oh, gosh I was so stupid! Maybe he had a wife!

He laughed so hard I thought he would fall over. His laughter angered me, so I reached to slap him but I missed and slipped; he caught me before I hit the floor. He searched my face; he seemed sad, and then he kissed me and I didn't stop him. My tears were dripping into the kiss but we never stopped. He whispered to me, "How many times have you been hurt, Athena?" He held me close, but I felt a crack in the Hoover Dam and before it broke and the water show began, I quickly stopped playing the victim and stood up straight to face him.

Before I could speak he said, "I don't have a girlfriend silly. I just like my private life." He explained that the art world could be judgmental and although he was popular, he was still the new kid on the block and didn't want to be gossiped about. His eyes seemed honest and as usual I felt like a fool. I was so used to being hurt that it was hard to recognize when a man was being genuine. I never stopped to consider that he could be telling the truth and that my little scene may have ruined his night.

A sly, skinny, greasy little man was trying his best to eavesdrop. Then he called Wyatt's name, "Smile Mr. Bretwater and say *cheese*." Snap, Snap, Snap went his camera. Wyatt was holding my hand to calm me, which was soothing considering the tantrum I just threw. He took a deep breath and said," Athena we will be on the cover of tomorrow's *Art Social*." I sheepishly smiled," Yeah the new up-and-coming golden boy of New York's art elite and his new *spazzed* out lady friend." I felt terrible, but Wyatt joked around and said, "Who knows? Maybe we'll get a reality show."

I went to the ladies' room to dry my face and collect my thoughts. I stayed there for a while, wrestling with my emotions. Maybe it was the wine. Why did I go off like that? It seemed to me that I was dealing with a massive storm on the inside of me. I never stopped to think about the harm I was doing myself by not healing the wounds of past disappointments. I almost erupted like a 9.3 magnitude quake. Wyatt didn't deserve that; we barely knew each other. I needed to deal with my crap. I noticed an elderly woman in the waiting area watching me. I felt she knew what I was thinking. Maybe she too had these thoughts; maybe some man had caused her trouble. The mystery women exposed me with one look. She smiled and nodded at me in an understanding way, and I knew that she could see it. I reapplied my lipstick and walked back through the crowd that had since calmed; everyone had resumed their own conversations. Wyatt ordered more red wine, which was probably a bad idea and we made fun of the snooty art curators.

The event was winding down and more and more people were spilling into the streets and going off to other destinations. This was the city that never sleeps. Wyatt left me a couple of times to shake hands and take photos. I watched the women watch him and I knew that they were doing that wedding-planning-in-their-heads-thing that we women do. Wyatt was definitely husband material. Once he finished working the room, we left and found ourselves in front of Rouge. We were leaning against the window chatting and still very much into the moment. I could tell something was happening between us but I also knew I had too much going on. ***Does anyone still believe in love at first sight? I wondered if Wyatt was the one that was made just for me.***

We shared a cab and surprisingly he didn't live too far from the Ansonia. He said the museum director suggested a boutique-style condo near Broadway in case he wanted to take in some theatre. We chatted some more, and the cab driver kept smiling at us. I thought about how many life experiences these cab drivers saw on a daily basis.

Before he got out he kissed my forehead again and he said, "Athena prayer lifts heavy loads and I'm living proof of it." As I watched him walk away, I wondered what kind of prayer peaceful Wyatt from Wyoming could ever need. I smiled all the way back to the Ansonia; the night was messy but still perfect.

Working Girl

The next day I woke up in bliss. I had the most peaceful dream of Wyatt. We were sitting under an apple tree in the middle of nowhere and green grass surrounded us. Wyatt painted while I read and from time to time we would smile over stolen glances but we never spoke a word. He kept painting and I kept reading. The memory of this dream made me wonder why I met him and what he would become to me. Was he just passing through? Was he the teacher and I the student or would it be the other way around? I got out of bed and greeted God with a smile and said, "Good morning." I felt silly saying good morning to the ceiling. I mean it's not like he would say, "Good Morning Athena." As soon as I said good morning it was as if the words good morning were imprinted in my heart and I knew today would be a good day. I was starting to get use to God responding to me no matter how silly I felt. Was I tripping or was Nan up there asking our creator to give me double Grace because she knew I would need it?

I grabbed my phone and headed to the kitchen to find it empty. Hmmm. This was strange for a Monday morning; no dark roast; no Kristen and no Gary. I guess they decided to sleep in, so I started to make my own coffee but the coffee maker frightened me. Why couldn't they own a normal coffee pot? This thing made coffee, espresso and cappuccino and you could probably bake a cake on it if you tried. I was determined to make a cup of coffee for myself and this gadget was not going to get the best of me. I searched online for the instructions and to my surprise someone was calling me from a 212 number. What kind of person dials another person at 5:00 am? I instantly felt uncomfortable and I knew this had to be Gerald. I watched the number on my screen, adjusted myself and picked up.

"Good Morning, Gerald, how can I help you this early?"

"May I speak with Athena Davenport please?" This voice didn't sound familiar. Ok, so it wasn't Gerald, but now I was nervous; the person on the other end sounded so serious.

"This is she," I said. The mystery person was the casting director for *Paradise on Earth Organics*. This was the new organic hair care commercial I had auditioned for. I knew the director liked me, but I never thought he would call me back. She went on to explain that call time was today at 12 noon. I was to show up with a plain face and comfortable shoes.

Her name was Susan and she spoke in that snooty no-nonsense, I- can-make-or-break-your-life kind of tone. I listened carefully to her instructions and she ended the call with a cold, "Good luck" and then she was gone. She hung up on me while I was still thanking her but I didn't care. I stood there alone in the kitchen in shock and of course I started to cry. How could I be this terrified and excited at the same time? I could not believe that I had booked a job on my first shot in New York.
"Athena, you have the right to be here. You are brave and this is your time." I repeated that to myself almost 100

times before I moved a muscle. Then, I started screaming at the top of my lungs, "Thank you God, thank you God." I booked a job. I was screaming and jumping, jumping and screaming. I ran through the halls and back to the kitchen, crying and screaming. All of my dramatics woke Kristen and Gary, and they rushed into the kitchen.

Gary had a bat in his hand and Kristen was armed with a shoe. The sight of my sister holding a shoe caused me to hysterically laugh, and then she laughed and poor Gary lowered his bat in bewilderment.

"Athena, have you lost your damn mind?" Gary walked over and put his hand across my forehead. I had lost my voice. I was speechless; I stood there and watched them watch me. Then I blurted it out. "Ok, hold on to your socks. I actually booked a real job."

Kristen leaped in the air and rushed over to me screaming at the top of her lungs. "I'm so proud of you, thank God!"

Gary smiled, hugged me and said, "You deserve this, Sis."

Gary walked back to the bedroom and probably passed out; he looked so tired when he ran into the kitchen armed with a baseball bat. Kristen worked her fancy coffee maker and we spent the next couple of hours going over the details of my first job.

Time seemed to be on fast forward from this morning's excitement and I was ready to go. I finally pulled up to a bricked building in Greenwich Village at 11:30 am. I was early, but I felt nauseous. I didn't know how I was going to get through this day with these nerves but I forced one foot in front of the other and I wobbled my butt through the front door. I walked into a busy scene. Leggy girls of all colors bobbed and weaved in and out of different rooms. The girls had hair clips and pins hanging out of their unfinished heads. Everyone seemed to know exactly where they were supposed to be. Susan had explained that I was to look for the sign that said *Hair and Makeup* and give my name to her assistant. I followed the leggy girls back to the main room, but no one was around. I took a few deep breaths and waited and waited and then waited some more. I started to panic because it was now 11:55 am and I didn't see anyone that looked like an assistant.

"Um, H-e-l-l-o," he said with an attitude; he startled me.

"Hello, my name is, uh."

He cut me off in mid sentence and did a snap-finger-teeth-suck-stomp-off. Great! So far I had managed to upset this fashionable, man with my mere presence.

"I know who you are Ms. Late. Now follow me." He waved his hand behind his head in a gesture to get me to pick up the pace and walk faster. His designer neck scarf flapped behind him and I had to sprint to keep up with his tiny legs; whoa he was a little man. He rocked a perfect bob; he had perfect skin and he had the perfect jaw line.

His name was Isaac and he was Susan's temperamental assistant and I decided against telling him that I was actually on time. Something told me that I would get thrown out if I mentioned it. He stopped out of nowhere, and I almost ran into him.

"Here honey this is where you park it." Isaac handed me paperwork to fill out and walked off without another word.

I introduced myself to a chubby blond with a warm smile and spiked hair; her face was fully made up and I knew she would work her gift on me today. Her name was Stella and she explained that since this was a natural hair care commercial, I would be getting a style called the *Twist Out*. She was going to wash and condition my hair with *Paradise on Earth* and twist every strand of my hair with their famous Honey Dew Melon Gel, which was made of real honey dew.

I felt that old friend anxiety kicking in, so I tried to calm myself.

"Oh baby, don't look so worried. Susan is hard on Isaac, so Isaac is hard on the girls." Stella also explained that the Twist Out would take an hour or more and yes it would hurt but the trick was to act as if I felt perfectly fine. Oh yes acting. Well, that is why I came to New York in the first place, right? As I clenched the arms of Stella's chair in excruciating pain; I wondered how many times in life I had put on this show?

Hmmm, let's see. I had acted as if I liked every one of Reece's get-rich-quick schemes. I acted as if I were fine with the way Antonio shouted at me; I even acted as if I enjoyed my soul-sucking job and the fact that Gerald was so demanding. ***How many times had we walked around in pain acting as if everything was just fine but we were secretly dying inside?*** I guess if you think about it, most of us were already Stellar Award winning actresses, and today I decided to suck it up just as I had many times before and put on my game face. I relaxed a little more, smiled, unclenched the sides of the chair and started talking with Stella.

The other girls all proclaimed to be model slash actresses and questioned me about what agency I came from. I was just a self-proclaimed beginner trying to make her way. Each and every time I explained that I didn't have an agency I got the same shocked reaction. Apparently all the girls were represented by some fancy agency and the fact that I walked right in off the streets annoyed most of them. Stella gave me tips on keeping that to myself because it might threaten some of the girls. After about an hour and thirty minutes I stood up and looked in the mirror. I laughed out loud because I looked like that killer alien in that movie *The Predator.* I always seem to laugh at the most inopportune times and everyone turned to see what was so funny and that everyone included Isaac. His cold little eyes pierced through me. Where did he come from?

"Shall I tell Susan the joke that made you interrupt our preparations?" Oh gosh, my face felt hot and I didn't know how to respond. I couldn't get fired from my first real job. Stella walked close to me, grabbed my hand and said, "Oh Isaac, it was an insider and keep this one close because she's special." I let out a huge sigh of relief and Stella winked at me. "Don't let him chew you out. God will see you through," she said.

Isaac snatched the forms out of my hand and gestured for me and a few of the other girls to follow him to the next chair. As I walked away I turned and smiled at Stella—what a kind and yet strange thing to say on the set of a commercial. I always thought these kind of industry, self-absorbed people kept God out of everything. I remembered something that Nan would always say: "God has people and he will touch hearts to get you to the right places, if you believe." Was Stella one of God's people? Was I one of God's people? Maybe I was thinking way too deep on this one. I would never forget Stella and we did cross paths again.

We reached another room and makeup was everywhere; we took our seats and waited for our makeup wizards. Isaac handed us the slides that we were to memorize in the next fifteen minutes. I overheard some of the girls complaining about how that was not enough time, but I didn't say a word. You see I had taken many memorization classes on YouTube and those techniques kicked in.

I sat in the chair and got painted, plucked and smooshed into a different person and I tried my best to go over my lines. The makeup artist seemed annoyed; she wasn't as kind as Stella, so I kept the small talk to a minimum. After about 30 minutes, Isaac came back in yelling about being behind schedule. I opened my eyes as she spun me around and I prepared myself. I had already made a mental note not to laugh, but this was no laughing matter. *I was breathtaking.* I examined myself in the mirror a little longer than I should have and I knew I probably looked liked a newbie, but I didn't care. I was the girl who came to New York afraid and I was looking at myself in the mirror and it started to sink in that I actually had the right to be here.

Another girl came back to untwist my hair and put the finishing touches on the rest of the girls. The preparations were over and we started walking down a long corridor to the set. All of the girls appeared over confident as they sashayed onward and I had to concentrate on not tripping over my own feet. Once we reached the set I was blown away; there were four different stages, and they all had different colored backdrops. There was gold for the goddess, white for the sophisticate, black for the powerful and purple for royalty. The sets had different props and each model was assigned to a background color that went with the hair and makeup.

The sounds of the camera's clicking and the director's words had me on a natural high.

"Okay, ladies we will run it a few times. I need high energy and give me hair excitement." I was pleased to find out that the director was the happy man that squealed over my hair during the audition. He walked over to me, kissed me on both cheeks and I got a glimpse of the creators of the hair care line.

For a split second I was stuck, enamored by a grace I have never seen on women before. The proud look on the director's face confirmed my suspicions. I gazed in amazement at the queens that appeared before me. I think they were twins like me and Kristen or sisters that looked a lot alike. Their long slender legs peeked out of the slits in their vintage skirts. They had full pouty lips, thick dark eyebrows and big wild hair just like mine. They were intimidating and soft at the same time and very young to be powerhouse business women.

The sight of the Quan Sisters fueled my energy and there was a shift in me. It was that same shift I felt in my first class when I stepped inside of the circle and went free. It was as if the true me took over, and I became a confident, professional; Dear God Thank you. Isaac directed me to go over to the all black set first and then he directed me to the purple set; I was greeted by the assistant director and the camera man. I went over my lines once more and stepped into my new comfort zone.

"Hey ladies, are you over dry brittle hair? Well let me show you what you've been missing with POE Organics." I pranced and posed and swung my soft twists for the camera. Wow this stuff was amazing and my hair felt so soft.

The director smiled and had me go over my lines once more and then that was a wrap. I shot the commercial and a few promo photos in two takes. Cipriani and Theodora Quan walked over to me and personally invited me to work on their next project; they reeked of the cool and trendy. How could two women be this--I don't even know what to call them--incredible and very kind. It took everything in me not to hug them and ask to hang out. I pushed the dork deep inside and calmly accepted the invitation. I could hardly contain my excitement. I could not believe they were thanking me for my good work.

I noticed Isaac trying to get into our conversation, but the girls paid him no mind. He kept finding his way into my space and I wondered what he wanted from me.

He was acting like a lonely alley cat cozying up to me until we were brushing arms. This was weird.

"So I knew you weren't late," he said in an apologetic tone. I was shocked. This little jerk had admitted that he was testing me and he actually watched me walk in early and wonder around in confusion. I didn't find his prank funny, but I held my composure and thanked him for the opportunity. I knew it was the director and Susan who chose me, but Stella had explained that he was Susan's second assistant, so I figured he probably needed kindness more than I did. I walked out of the brick building with the mother of all headaches from my twists but even that wasn't going to get me down. As my hair blew in the wind I imagined myself becoming strong and powerful. I didn't realize at the time that I already was.

I was in the mood to roam Greenwich Village, but it was getting dark and I needed food. This would be a great time to call Daniel, because he knew the best places to eat in any part of New York. I really missed Daniel, but there was still some weirdness between us. I thought about calling Wyatt, but I decided that it might be too soon so I decided to have dinner by myself. My insides where smiling and I thanked God for this day. I looked across the street and my stomach lead me to a cozy Asian noodle spot that was actually called *Noodle Spot*. I stepped off the curb to cross the street and smacked right into the passenger door of an SUV. It happened so fast that my arm was throbbing and I was pissed. Some drivers had no regard for human life.

"Hey are you trying to kill me?" I yelled and waved my sore arm as if I were one of those tough, new Yorkers. The SUV slowly pulled up on the curb and I got quiet. Ok maybe it was time for me to calm down. I started having flash backs of *Law and Order* and I got the urge to run. I was all bark and no bite and now I was a nervous wreck.

The black tinted window slowly started to come down. "Now why would I ever harm a head on your head?" It was Gerald! How did he know where I was? Did he follow me? Was this just a coincidence? Ok, Athena prepare yourself. I guess it's time you faced him.

"Hey Gerald you really should test your driver's eyesight; he almost took my arm off." That's it, Athena! I ignored the big, pink elephant standing on the corner with me, because I was not ready to discuss the fact that I have been avoiding him.

Gerald looked different. I'd never seen him in jeans and sneakers, and he seemed softer and less empowered. He stepped out and walked in my personal space as he often did; he grabbed my hands, and he was shaking. I could still feel something between us; he was still in my system. I gently pulled my hands away. I needed to tell him that this wasn't going to happen.

"Athena you have been ignoring my gifts and calls for almost a month." Here we go. I had to get ready for this. I had been so caught up in me that four days turned into four weeks. This had to be the Universe forcing me to deal with him. I told him that after our last conversation I needed space to figure out some things and to focus on the main reason I came here. He didn't respond well to this, and he seemed so weak. Something else had to be wrong. "Is everything ok Gerald?"

He had a sad blank stare and he said that his mother died. She had been ill and died during my hideout and also the board was trying to remove him from one of his biggest companies. He leaned his head on my shoulder and I could feel his heaviness. I really felt bad for him and the natural thing for me to do was to cradle him in my arms and that's exactly what I did. I was stunned at his reaction; he was whimpering and I didn't have the heart to tell him I didn't want to see him anymore.

After pleading with me to meet him for dinner tomorrow I reluctantly agreed. We stood on the corner for a little while longer. He asked me where I was coming from as he eyed my hair so I told him. He didn't seem too happy for me although he said he was proud of me. He did manage to smile and say he would contact an agent that owes him a favor and set up a meeting for me. The thought of having an actual agent in New York sent me soaring through the clouds. I still had that little pain in my gut that told me to decline his offer but I chose to ignore it.

"Great we can talk about it over dinner tomorrow night," he said. He offered to drive me back to the Ansonia but I stood my ground and said no. I had my heart set on being alone and eating those noodles. He leaned in for a kiss and I didn't have the heart to completely turn away so I turned slightly and we ended up in an awkward chin kiss. I knew this would upset him so I quickly back away before he could try again and waved good bye.

I walked across the street and purposely walked passed the noodle place; I didn't want him following me so I kept walking and looking back until the SUV pulled off. The tiny noodle placed didn't disappoint. The scent of that soy sauce saturated the air and made my stomach growl. I had two servings of Dan-Dan noodles that were so good I started wiggling my toes around in my boots. Wiggling my toes is something I have always done when I had a great meal; I don't know why it's just a thing of mine. I sat at that table lost in my thoughts about my future and after a while I realized I had lost track of time because the night crowd started to pour in and pack the place.

The Lesson

The next morning I woke up feeling so accomplished that I stood up and started jumping on the bed.

"Who is the big cheese up in here?" I screamed.

Kristen rushed in and found me jumping on the bed, she took off her slippers and jumped with me.

"You're the big cheese!" she yelled.

We collapsed onto the bed in laughter. She hugged me and we sat there enjoying the moment. Kristen suggested that we call Teresa, so we dialed our mother and put her on speaker.

"Hello Mummy," we giggled in a fake accent the way we did when we were little.

I was already prepared to hear every reason why Kristen should move back home and why I should give up auditioning. Teresa paused for a second and I thought she hung up and then she said: "Girls, you are becoming my teachers." She was crying.

What was happening to us?

She talked about working on her own dreams and how this was her time. Who was this lady and what did she do with my fearful mother? After we hung up with Teresa, we dialed the girls and let the news go. We all screamed and the girls called me *Ms. Hollywood.* In all this excitement I couldn't help but think of Daniel. Kristen stayed with me, and we lay side by side staring at her ceiling, and I knew what we were both thinking: Fear has no place here and it is time for the final eviction process to begin. We ended up lying in bed for another hour until Gary came. He was flustered.

"Girls come quickly, you have to see this."

We rushed to the kitchen to see what all the fuss was about. To my surprise the counter was covered in gift boxes and roses.

"Whose birthday is it?" He looked annoyed. "Apparently it's yours."

"No way." I was in shock. Gary explained that they were left at the concierge's desk. They were addressed to me and the manager was no longer willing to let them sit there or to give them away. Gary was told that if he didn't take them, he would be fined. Kristen and I carefully opened each box; there was a satin dress, a silk dress, a few sparkling dresses, a fur shawl, a diamond necklace and two designer purses.

The little butterflies danced inside, but the sensible part of me knew better. ***Why is it that there is always a final test?*** I had never had a man pamper me this way, but I knew I couldn't keep any of this. I explained to them that I agreed to meet Gerald for dinner.

Gary was not happy about these gifts. "Athena this is too much, and who is this guy?" Gary broke the man code by explaining that when men try to buy women, usually it's because they have hidden motives.

Could gifts really harm me?

"Kristen, what do you think?" he asked.

My sister was too busy twirling in my shawl to be a productive part of this conversation and Gary seemed annoyed with her.

"Hello earth to my-soon-to-be ex-wife." He snapped his fingers, and she broke out of her trance and she took off the shawl.

Kristen said it seemed premature to buy these gifts and reminded me why I was avoiding him in the first place. She also reminded me that I had made dinner plans with them and one of Gary's partners. I felt bad for blowing it off, but I wanted to talk with Gerald about the agent, to explain my feelings about not dating him and to return the gifts. Kristen seemed disappointed, but I knew she would get over it.

I spent the rest of the day looking for auditions and talking on the phone with the girls because of course they called back to hear more about my first job; I really had the best friends.

The evening came quickly and I started the process of getting all dolled up for Gerald, but I kept checking my phone waiting for Daniel to call. He was the only one I didn't share the news with and I decided enough was enough. I missed my friend, so I dialed his number; it rang for half a second and he picked up.

"Hello dear," his voice was cheerful and I could tell he was happy that I called.

I gave him the news about the job and apologized for being a bad friend. He screamed like Kristen did and I started laughing. He didn't ask to see me to celebrate which was odd, so I found myself asking him about his plans. I could tell he didn't want to answer me, and then he informed me that he had a date with Ginger from the Impromptu Class. My face got hot. What was going on with me? I didn't want Daniel romantically—or did I? I concealed my jealously and congratulated him. "Liar," he said and we burst out laughing. We agreed to catch up the next day for lunch.

I went with the strapless, black sparkling number, black stiletto pumps, the fur shawl and the diamond necklace. I gave myself a once over in the foyer. I could hear Kristen and Gary whistling at me, "Whoa, momma," they teased.

Gary gave me a serious look and said, "Tell him no more gifts." Kristen rubbed Gary's back to sooth him; he was overly protective; I had the brother I always wanted. He instantly calmed down and scooped her off her feet and kissed her. Yes-they were back into each other and out of my business.

At that time it didn't dawn on me but Kristen had found herself and Gary by spending time with God and they both seemed to be at peace. I excused myself from their make out session and walked out of the door and into the elevator. The elevator ride seemed normal, so I took this as a sign that it would be a good night. I walked through the lobby and watched as heads turned in my direction and I felt famous. Gerald was waiting with flowers. Wow, this guy was really going for it! Once I reached the car door he pulled me close and tried to kiss me. This didn't feel natural, and I wanted to turn around. He had this strange look in his eye—it was half deranged wolf and half puppy.

"You know I'm really hoping that you want to be all mine."

Ok. This date was moving at the speed of light and I needed some air. I cracked the window and let the cold air slice the thick heat that was radiating off of him. I said I'd consider his offer. Why did I lie? I had no intention of considering his offer. I could tell my answer upset him because he did that jaw tightening thing that Daniel did.

I started thinking about Daniel and his hot date. I wondered if he was really going for it and was she special to him. Did he bring her flowers?

The car pulled up to one of Gerald's penthouses at 7338 Park Avenue. And just as I expected, this place was incredible. I was a little confused about why we had to stop here, but he said it was important, so I agreed. We were escorted by security through a private entrance and once we were on the elevator, my ears began to pop as we kept going higher and higher. The doors opened and I could feel the pulse in my aching temples. I was nervous and I had every right to be; I just stepped into another world. The butler was waiting to take my shawl and he handed Gerald a cigar. I didn't know he smoked; I hated smoke and I made a mental note to talk with him about the dangers of smoking. He bragged about the crystal chandelier that he had imported from France; he said it once belong to one of the royal families. He had rare African artifacts and ancient art all around this place.

He took my hand and walked me past a grand piano where a young woman was seated; her fingers must have been blessed by God because she played a melody that soothed my nerves and I started to calm down.

I asked Gerald what was so important. He explained that we were having dinner here and that he had hired a chef to cook for us.

I was starting to think he didn't like people. What was with this guy and the private dinners? I noticed that same puppy look was back in his eyes and I was praying he didn't propose marriage. Why do I always get myself in these situations? ***Does anyone else have a self-destructive pattern that needs to be severed at the root?***

"Athena you could share my world, if you wanted to—I want you."

Oh no. If this dude proposes, I would be so out of here. I could jump off the balcony, but I quickly assessed the risk and knew I would not survive. While I was mentally planning my escape, I noticed him coming closer and closer until there was no space between us. My mouth went dry and I started shaking; my feet wouldn't move. What was going on with me? He tried to kiss me again, but this time, before I could move, he held the back of my neck. My heart was racing, but it wasn't out of passion; it was out of fear.

I needed to get away from him and to tell him the reason that I agreed to dinner, but instead I did as he instructed and began our three-course dinner. Another woman walked over to the heated balcony where we were seated and handed me a glass of red wine. She looked at me with such pity; what had I done to her?

Mini fire pits blazed on his balcony which was a large lounge area. I started to get warm as I took in the view and sipped the wine. I let my mind go free as I began to relax. The salad was mixed with beautiful colored peppers and olive oil dressing.

I reached for a piece of bread and Gerald lightly slapped my hands, "No let me." He was so controlling. I couldn't even get my own bread, so I let him feed it to me. The woman returned and handed me another glass of wine; I was tipsy before the main course arrived. I let my guard down and we laughed as he listened to the details of my first big job.

I could hear those magic fingers playing that soothing melody, so I took off my shoes and stood up to dance. I felt sexy and a little too free; this was totally out of character. I reached for his hand and I saw pure wolf in his eyes; the little puppy was gone. We started dancing to the melody but he wanted to slow down so he grabbed my hips and started rotating them towards him. I was giddy.

"Athena, I searched years for a woman like you and you will be mine."

I laughed at him; he really needed to relax. "Sir, yes sir," I said saluting him as if I were a cadet in the army. This upset him, but I couldn't stop laughing and before I knew it we were walking away from the balcony and into his bedroom. He held me close and again we danced, but this time I could not hear the music. He whispered all kinds of life plans in my ear such as, how I was to be as his wife, how I was to dress and who I would be allowed to see. I jokingly agreed but the look on his face said this was no laughing matter. Something was off with his demeanor.

And then it happened. I could feel him slowly unzipping my dress, and that's when I stopped laughing, but I felt like I was in a fog. Man how much did I really have to drink? My legs felt heavy. I made a mental note to lay off the wine.

"Gerald I thin, I-I-I shou go humb,ok. . . ." What the heck was I saying? I felt like that character from Charlie Brown, Wah- Wah- Wah- Wah. I couldn't find the correct words, and now he was laughing but he was angry; this was so confusing.

I tried walking away to find my shoes, but I felt like I was stuck in quicksand. His room was large and unfamiliar and every time I looked for the exit there was another room.

How could someone's bedroom have so many rooms? In my mind I was walking around his room looking for an exit, but when I looked down, I saw that I had not moved. I stood in that same spot.

"It is not okay that you leave, you ungrateful slut!" His voice was wicked and numb. My eyes started tearing up because I was afraid. Ok, I was trapped in the terror dome, shoeless and purse-less, which meant I had no access to my phone and apparently my legs had stopped working; this was a freaking nightmare. He came up behind me and starting taking off my dress; again I tried to face him but I could not move. I even tried yelling, but I couldn't find my voice and before I could try again, my dress was around my ankles and in one quick move my panties and bra had been removed. I felt sick. I told him to stop, but it made him worse.

When he looked at me, he was different and I could tell that Gerald was gone. I didn't know who I was alone with. I thought I saw the walls breathing; my head was spinning and then lightning struck. I tried to scream at the tops of my lungs, but no sound came out. The pain was so unbearable that I fell to the floor. It took a second for me to realize that Gerald was standing over me screaming, calling me the vilest of names.

Ok, it just got real and in this moment I realized that all Daniel tried to do was protect me. Gerald had beat his ex-wife and I would be victim number two or three—who knew how many others there had been. So many thoughts ran through my mind. Would I survive the night? Why did his ex-wife stay for so long and why was I here with him in the first place? I tried to stand, but I couldn't, so he helped me up, but my legs were like wet noodles. He threw me like a rag doll and I went crashing across his floor head first. Blood spattered and I thought I would die there.

"*You are mine!*" he screamed. Spit flew out of the corners of his mouth. He said he followed me to that dirty coffee shop and saw me with that piece of nothing pretty boy. Ok Athena, this was really happening. He had been following me and deep down inside I think I knew it. **Why don't we trust our instincts?** All I could feel was regret.

"No woman of mine will be seen in a hole in the wall with some worthless artist!" he roared.

 He had me by one arm and lightening struck again; he banged my head on the floor and I heard a crunching sound; I think my nose was broken but that was the least of my worries. I was woozy; I could taste my blood as it ran down the side of my face. Oh God, he was going to kill me. I could not scream for help, and I knew he would get away with it because he was rich and powerful. I had nothing and no one in this moment. But then something happened, and I thought of my Nan and I knew exactly what to do.

I began to mumble the Lord's Prayer, "Our father who art in Heaven, hollowed be thy name, thy kingdom come thy will be done." I mumbled The Lord's Prayer as Nan taught me and each time I mumbled, lightning struck. He hit me so many times I could no longer feel the pain but somehow I could still pray.

He drew his fist back to hit me again and I was sure the last blow would finish me. He paused and looked at me; he actually looked sorry; he picked my lifeless body off of the floor and started weeping.

"I'm sorry, Athena, I'm sorry Mommy." This guy was nuts. Why was he calling me *Mommy*?

I had no strength; I started to lose conscientiousness. In my mind I was saying good-bye to my sister, my best friends and everyone I had ever loved. The tears rushed out of my swollen eyes seeping into my wounds. He stopped weeping and then everything got quiet; the lightening stopped; everything stopped. The panic settled in.

No, no was I dead? I heard a door open and a muffled scream. I thought it was the woman who gave me the wine, but I couldn't make out her face, and then I fainted.

Throughout the ages of time, I'm sure many women have found themselves in dangerous situations as a result of not trusting their internal warnings. Nan would call that not trusting the Holy Spirit. The Grace of God is something that some will never accept, but it doesn't matter because God still gives it and then there will be others that will accept but never fully understand it and do what they want to do anyway. At that time I think I understood why Gerald didn't deliver that final blow. What made this girl walk into his bedroom? I'm sure she knew what could happen to her for interrupting.

Every encounter I had from the whisper on the roof top with Reese, to the gentle calm in the wind and even in the closet, I knew it; I think deep down I have always known God was trying to reach me; maybe to save me from myself and I pretended I wasn't sure instead of surrendering. *I wonder how many of us go through life pretending the strange things that happen to us are coincidences. Deep down inside do we know God is trying to get our attention?*

That night, fearful, as I lay on the floor in Gerald's arms, I was fully aware that love stepped in and saved my life, but the reason was unclear.

I woke up Saturday morning in Cornell Medical Center with Kristen, Gary and Daniel by my side. My jaw was broken in two places, my nose was broken, my ribs were cracked and I had lost two teeth. I had Rohypnol in my system which explains why I was dizzy. The doctors still couldn't figure out why I wasn't knocked out cold. My face was bruised and swollen, but I was alive. The doctors said I was still in shock; I had been going in and out of consciousness, but otherwise I would be fine.

"She's awake, she's awake." Daniel was so excited he kissed my hand and leaned over to hug me. I winced in pain but tried to smile; I didn't want to tell him he was being too rough. Kristen and Gary leaned in to talk to me, but I was embarrassed about everything, so I didn't say a word. Kristen explained that the chef and a few of Gerald's employees heard me scream and called the police. The woman that interrupted was afraid they wouldn't get there in time, so she decided to open the door. I will forever be grateful to her. Gerald is out on bail and his lawyers are claiming that I slipped from being too intoxicated and that I had taken some kind of party drug right before dinner; he also claimed witnesses saw me taking pills. My insides ached with anger because I knew he would get away with it. The woman that saved me disappeared that night, probably out of fear, and the staff and the chef were not talking. Just great! I was considered a bruised-up, pill-popping actress. What a cliché! I shook my head and Gary stopped Kristen from going into detail about the legalities. The mere mention of his name took me back to that night and I could not bear it.

I was released that next afternoon and Daniel begged Kristen and Gary to let him stay by my side and they agreed. Daniel slept on the floor by my bed every night for the next two weeks; he got up early with Kristen and Gary to make me coffee and even went to a few of my follow-up visits and dentist appointments. Gary made an appointment with a popular cosmetic dentist; Gary said I couldn't be an actress with missing teeth. I didn't have the heart to tell them I had lost all desire for Broadway and much of anything else. I couldn't look at myself in the mirror; I no longer felt proud or brave. I was lost and all I wanted to do was sleep.

I stayed in New York for another two months and Kristen tried to get me back to normal, but I freaked out every time a black SUV drove by or a middle-aged man in a power suit came near me. I finally lost my job back in

Philly, but I was okay with that. Gary had paid my rent for the next couple of months and I still had Nans money.

"Ok, I have some great news," Kristen said.

She giggled and said, "I am Mrs. Gary Whitaker." She squealed in excitement. How could she get married without me? Kristen revealed that they no longer wanted to wait, so one day after a lunch date they ran to the justice of the peace and secretly got hitched. They agreed it was best to push back the big ceremony until I was well enough to be apart of it.

Kristen was just full of surprises today. She said once I was ready she was going to come live with me in Philly and Gary agreed. The guilt started to kick in because I came into my sister's world and ruined all of her plans; it was time for me to go and I was going alone.

Going Back to Philly

It was Monday morning. Monday had come and gone so many times and I still wasn't ready to face life, but I had to go home. I still felt terrible for all the stress I put on Kristen and Gary. I quietly packed throughout the night and now here I was at 3:30 in the morning lying on my back in my sister's spare bedroom staring at the words on the ceiling. *Will I ever be limitless and free again?* I was embarrassed at the thought of crawling back to Philly with nothing but I missed home. Gerald had stolen my peace, and I wasn't sure if I would ever be the same, but I knew I had to fight for my life. I knew I had made bad choices and I knew I had to leave before Kristen and Gary got up. I lay there for a few more minutes; the tears rolled down the side of my face and soaked my hair. I slowly got up, looked around the room and found Nan's old Bible. I was about to leave it in the closet. I opened it and felt nothing.

I cried out, "Lord I have no peace!"

I skimmed around and noticed some of Nan's notes, so I stopped at John 14:27, "My peace I give you, my peace I leave with you, I do not give as the world gives, do not let your heart be troubled do not be afraid." My hands began to get warm, and it was as if the words were hugging my insides. I knew that God had answered me. I dropped the Bible on the floor and I dropped to my knees in tears. Nan had been right all along. I sat on the floor rocking myself, but I knew I was not alone. I was so hurt and although I knew I had God's peace it would be a while before I owned it. I collected myself, picked up the Bible, looked around the room and decided to never come back to New York. I left Kristen a note on the kitchen counter and crept out the front door. I called the front desk to have my old car ready. Once I saw her pull up, I was filled with joy; my car felt like Philly and I could not wait to get back home to everything that was comfortable to me.

I jumped in and hit the road. I rolled all the windows down; it was definitely the beginning of winter. I blew my breath in little o's and that's when I noticed the snow flurries, so pure and light, but I wouldn't allow myself to admit how beautiful the city looked. I finally reached the Holland Tunnel where it all began and I didn't look back. Two hours later I pulled up to the front of my cozy Chestnut Hill house. I was back home with Nan's money, no plan and all I wanted to do was pop my pain meds and sleep.

Wyatt texted me occasionally asking if he did something wrong, but I knew I could not explain this to him, so I responded that I had an emergency and had to go back home. I felt terrible for leaving him like that, and I wanted to keep in touch and see him again, but I couldn't.

The funny thing about chasing your dreams is that once you've had a small taste, you start to miss the high and it's hard to give them up. I was over sitting in my smelly pajama's ignoring everyone's calls and looking for boring office jobs I knew I couldn't take. My mind said it was time to get back to that brown, dismal cubicle life, but my spirit, although damaged, still wanted to soar to the stages of Broadway. Daniel sent me roses every Friday at

12 noon with a small card that said: *Your dreams are waiting*. Time can fly when you are stuck in depression, and it was finally time for me for me to step into my peace and stop feeling sorry for myself.

The girls finally decided to hold an intervention. Bang! Bang! BANG! "We know you're in there; we can see you." Yeah and we can smell you, Carmen yelled.

It took everything in me not to burst out in laughter. I really needed to shower. I sat on the couch and listened to my favorite people bang on my door. My heart smiled at how much those two loved me, and I knew I had to let them in. Was I ready to talk? Would they judge me? How could I explain this? I opened the door, and my girls flew in and Cynthia was with them. I wasn't prepared for another face, but I couldn't show it, and I did love little Cynthia.

Cynthia was fire and ice; she was the stronger version of Carmen and the baby of the two. I loved how she would put her hands on her tiny hips and widen her eyes as she boldly said, "A woman should never have to ask *why* and if he makes you wonder *why*, dump him because he's not the one!"

"Well little Cynthia, lately my life has been one big *why*, so I guess I may never find the one."

We stood there by the front door in a group hug; no words were spoken; there was silence and lots of tears. Judging by the girls' reactions, I knew that Kristen had informed them about that night so I wouldn't have to. The afternoon was filled with a much-needed shower, laughs, a little wine and Thai takeout from Lemon Grass, my favorite corner spot. The girls ended up staying the night and Mary wouldn't stop asking about my auditions.

"I can't believe you booked a real job out there," Mary said.

The room got quiet and the girls watched for my response. Mary had a way of being sneaky pushy as I call it. She knew New York conversations were off limits, and I knew this was her way of nudging me back there. Carmen stepped in to save me and handed me my phone which had been buzzing.

The number 212 flashed across the screen and I threw my phone and ran as fast as I could to the bathroom, but I didn't make it and up came my Shrimp Pad Thai all over my lilac-colored tiles. The girls followed me and stood there in disbelief; we all knew why I was upset, but we all remained silent. Carmen had tears in her eyes, and I think Mary had murder on her mind as she paced the halls in anger. And then sweet Cynthia said it, "Ok, tomorrow we are doing church and brunch."

The girls yelled, "*Hell no!*" at the same time, and I slammed the bathroom door. Was I ready to face God in his own house after what happened to me? He did tell me I had his peace, but I still felt guilty for being so stupid. I sobbed as I cleaned up my vomit, and again I wondered if I would ever be the same.

I knew I needed help and I knew I missed New York. Growing up little Cynthia always got what she wanted and this was no different, so I guessed I was going to church. Tomorrow morning we were going to The Love of Grace Church of God, with Pastor Rose Presley. Cynthia said this church had done amazing things for her life; she was newly married and starting her new job as a crime scene investigator and I could tell that Carmen was proud. Cynthia was always nosey so investigating was a perfect job for her. I decided to invite Teresa; she probably was worried and I missed her.

The girls left early so we could all get ready and meet at Cynthia's church. Teresa was here waiting for me. I was upstairs trying to think of an excuse to get out of going. I felt clammy and nervous. Would God be pissed at me for what happened with Gerald and for ignoring his warnings in New York? I really needed to talk with Nan. I went to tell Teresa I wasn't going and bumped right into her; she had been watching me go through the motions. She really was different. I never saw her wear confidence so well, but I wished she would stop staring at me.

"Tell me Athena, I need to hear it from you." We really didn't have time for this, so I gave her the short version, and when I was done she stood there with a blank expression, but I could see anger brewing and she frightened me. My mother was trembling and I could feel her rage. She grabbed my wrist and her red nails dug into my skin. Then she softly whispered "Let that be the last time."

I could see her fighting back tears and I knew she had experienced abuse at one point. Had my father been abusive or had it been another? I wondered about all the mothers that are hiding stories from their daughters still living in shame unwilling to be healed. We sat down on the bed and she held me in her arms. I whimpered like a child and she began to sing. I was shocked. She had a beautiful voice. In the past I would always catch her humming but then she'd stop and walk away. Her voice was strong like Pop's; maybe this was where I got it from. What other talents was she hiding? I felt safe in my mother's arms; we had never bonded like this.

We were thirty minutes late for the service, so we snuck in the back and got caught by a no-nonsense usher who seemed upset that we didn't ask her to seat us. She eyed us through her thick glasses and adjusted her wig before walking off. I made a mental note to never do that again. We ended up sitting next to Carmen and Mary; they were late as well. Cynthia was seated up front with her husband Paul; they were a beautiful couple. As I watched them I started to feel that one day that would happen for me—I'd find the right one.

The front of the church was a deep, royal purple and the colored stained glass gleamed and reminded me of the Byzantine period. The pastor's voice penetrated my heart; she shouted with conviction, "There is nothing that you could ever do that would make the father stop loving you!"

Huh, was she talking to me? Why was she staring at me and how could she see that far? I'm sure if she knew what happened in New York she would say something different. I looked down at my shoes and sang and clapped along with the choir. I tried my best to let those words sink in. How was it possible to have that kind of love? I let that thought linger for a while as I contemplated how this was possible. The service was coming to a close and I was coming undone; I knew I had to get out of there. I had turned to the girls and Teresa to say my goodbyes and then Pastor Rose called to anyone who wanted to know true unhindered love and I instantly froze. I wanted to run to the front, but my feet wouldn't move. I was sick of man's love, fake love, abusive love and I was even sick of my own love. I wished Pastor Rose would come and get me. Her voice got louder as she called one last time, "There are still a few more people, and the Lord is saying come!"

I wanted to yell, "Here I am!" I was afraid I would miss it and then I noticed *him* watching me. How could he be here? How was it possible?

He reached the front of my aisle and held his hand out to me and said, "Hello Ms. would you mind walking me to the front?"

The girls were watching with their mouths wide open, and Teresa was smiling. I was nervous, but I took his hand anyway. We walked hand in hand to the front of the church and Pastor Rose laid her hands on my forehead and began to pray; my insides were on fire. I finally stopped running from the one who loved me most.

I received an indescribable, deep-rooted love that swelled my heart and caused my knees to buckle there in front of everyone. Others were up there with me going through their own cleansing process. There was the rough-looking kid that untied his red bandanna and raised his lanky arms in surrender; there was a grown man that wailed like a baby in the arms of another church member that was ready and willing to hold him. Everyone was so full of love, and all I could feel was peace and I knew this had to be from God.

People started heading back to their seats, but he was still holding my hand. My eyes were puffy; I'm sure my mascara was smeared all over my face and my nose was snotty, but I didn't care, and apparently neither did he. He smiled at me and my thoughts flashed to the day he gave me a ticket, and then I thought of how I cranked-called him and I started cracking up. He laughed with me even though he had no idea why I was laughing.

Kendrick Ryan faced me and we stood eye to eye. He was a golden brown and I'm sure he had been kissed by an island sunrise at least once in his life. His lashes looked like they were fighting for space to cover his eyelids and his knuckles were lightly dusted with hair. And yes his almond-shaped face and big brown eyes were kind. He was beautiful but it was more than physical although he was very attractive. His spirit was beautiful like Wyatt's.

After the service Kendrick introduced me to Pastor Rose and I was surprised to find out that this was his home church. And what were the odds of him and Cynthia's husband being friends. Pastor Rose held me in her arms and I could tell she was the real deal.

She smiled from her soul and whispered, "Women are God's rare jewels, be mindful of that." Her words saturated my insides and I started to feel that fire again. This was no ordinary church and I knew I had to return. The last of the congregation made their way out the front and Teresa and the girls waved good-bye. Eventually, no one was left but Kendrick and me. We walked over to the front pew and sat down; for some reason I couldn't face him, so I kept my eyes fixed on the floor until he lifted my chin with his index finger. We sat there face to face; what did he want from me? I watched him study me.

The stained glass windows behind me were beautiful, and I started to feel that peace that surpasses all human understanding. I was a wreck; I had been attacked; I had no job, no certainties and yet in this moment I kind of wanted to jump for joy; I had never felt so whole.

He smiled at me. He seemed nervous as he said, "Imagine seeing you here."

Of all the people I thought I would see in church, Kendrick never crossed my mind; God was definitely up to something.

"So you know Cynthia?" I asked. He laughed at my attempt to be cool and asked me if I wanted to take a walk to get some fresh air. Thank God. I couldn't take him staring at me a second longer.

He reached out toward my face, and then he stopped and said, "Um, you might want to check your face before we go."

Oh no, my face. I was sure I looked like I walked through a car wash; I felt sweaty and my hair was frizzy. The church bathroom smelled of rose and mint and the wall paper looked exactly how a church bathroom wall paper should look, calming and full of tranquil looking flowers. They even had artificial flowers in vases on both corners of the mirrors and boxes of Kleenex everywhere. Churches were always prepared for criers such as myself. I gave myself a once over in the mirror; yikes I had no words to describe what I looked like. I grabbed my magic makeover bag, the one every woman carries in her purse for emergencies. After fifteen minutes of spraying, wiping, and reapplying, I was a new woman. I gave myself a few sprays of *Lady Bug* and collected my thoughts before I walked out of the bathroom and back to see Kendrick. We walked out of the church the same way we walked to the front; hand in hand. Once the front doors opened, the sun blinded us and the winter air stung my cheeks; I felt so alive. I hadn't given much thought to Christmas until I noticed the decorated houses across the street. We walked through the residential neighborhood that surrounded the church. We talked about why he became an officer. We shared a few laughs about the night he gave me a ticket. I knew I would see him again. This was no coincidence.

I spent the next couple of weeks getting to know the real me. I kept myself busy with anything that would take my mind off of New York. I still couldn't bring myself to search for another office job, so I took a part-time job at a coffee café called, *Five Points* and it turned out that I was a handy little *barista*. I enjoyed people watching, picking up audition techniques from the regular actors, chatting with the older couples and serving holiday cookies. I even invited my favorite elderly couple over for my Christmas dinner and tonight was the night. I started packing away the condiments and cleaning the counter like a pro.

My phone started ringing, so I reached for it and the extreme panic kicked in. Those frightening feelings came crashing down and there it was again—another 212 area code. He was stalking me. I knew it was him, but I knew I couldn't let him break me. I broke out into a sweat. I was about to run and throw up, but I heard the bell on the front door jingle; I had forgotten to put the *Closed* sign up.

"Hey, I thought I would pop in and surprise you. Is this a bad time?"

This was terrible timing but I couldn't tell him that.

"Hello Kendrick. No it's not a bad time." I swallowed the lump of whatever was trying to come up and tried my best to remain calm. Kendrick rushed over to the sink, wet a paper towel and started wiping my forehead. I guess he was trained to spot BS, and he knew I wasn't fine but he never asked why. He grabbed the mop and spent the next half hour silently helping with the cleaning, and I knew I was safe with him. After he rescued me I decided to return the favor by inviting him to Christmas dinner. I wrote down

my address and he waited while I locked up; he even
waited for me to pull out of the parking lot; he was such a
gentleman.

I rushed home full of excitement. I had never hosted a
dinner at my house and I wanted everything to be perfect.
Once I got home I went into full Susie–homemaker mode. I
had candles burning and red trimming twisted around the
banister and my tree was perfect. I always remembered
what Nan said, "When it comes to Christmas, more is never
enough and don't forget the sparkle."

I played Donny Hathaway's "This Christmas," through my
speakers and a Patsy Cline version of "Silent Night," which
was Teresa's favorite. My store-bought turkey was freshly
carved. I was still too intimidated to cook a turkey, but I
was proud that I had made all the side dishes. I wore Nan's
silver-fitted sequenced dress and it felt good to get dolled
up again. I kept this dress in the back of the closet for
special occasions.

The girls began to bang uncontrollably on the door as they
normally did and I knew tonight would be great.

"*Hola Chica!*" they yelled. This was how we normally
greeted each other after spending nights at Carmen's when
we were little. I opened the door to see my girls and they
looked stunning. I never told them to wear sparkly dresses,
but we always did have that mind reading thing going on
when it came to fashion; we looked like an updated version
of the Supremes. Meredith went straight to pouring wine
before everyone else arrived.

"Athena, I want to toast to *new beginnings*." We smiled and they sipped their wine and I sipped my sparkling cider. I promised myself to lay off the wine and find a new way to deal with my emotions. And then I heard another knock at the door. I swung the door open and said, "Enter please." I startled poor Milton and Kay, the elderly couple that I befriended from the Five Points; Kendrick was right behind them. His face was frozen in shock. Every other time we met I was a crying mess.

He straightened his tie and took a deep breath. "Wow you're beautiful," he said, but before I could thank him Carmen grabbed him by the arm pulling him out of the cold, and Mary said in a coy manner, "Oh, you're quite welcome." We all started laughing, but he couldn't take his eyes off me.

A few seconds later Teresa walks in with a male friend that I had never seen. She also brought a few cousins that I didn't invite, but I was fine with their coming. I had never seen my mother with a man; she was definitely different; she walked past me and winked; well this was going to be an interesting night. We were still waiting for Kristen and Gary. Everyone was engrossed in conversation and enjoying the music. Kendrick and I watched each other as I filled glasses with iced tea and repositioned coasters. I heard a light tap on the door; finally they were here and we could eat.

When I opened the door I was floored. "Surprise!" My sister yelled and gave me a half sorry and half uncomfortable look.

Daniel wrapped me in his arms and lifted me off of the floor and nuzzled the side of my neck; he smelled amazing. I had missed him.

"God, Athena, you look well."

Daniel made this night go from interesting to awkward. Why didn't Kristen tell me she was bringing him? Why didn't he tell me he was coming? My sister and I had texted that morning. Gary hugged me and got out of the line of fire as I eyed Kristen.

Meredith had that troublesome grin plastered on her face as she said, "Hey, Hey, Hey! Now this is going to be fun."

Carmen threw a napkin at her, "Oh shut up, Mary." I ushered everyone into the dinning room for introductions. Daniel eyed Kendrick and Kendrick eyed Daniel and I stood by my so dead sister on the other side of the table. I asked Teresa to bless the food. Everyone bowed their heads as my mom prayed. My separate prayer went something like this, "Lord, please get Kristen later for this; please show me who the one is and please let this night go well, Amen." And just as Nan always told me, God did honor my prayer but not the way I thought he would. ***Has anyone ever realized that God's ways of doing things are totally different from our ways?*** His plans for us are so much bigger than we could have ever imagined. Everyone loved my store-bought turkey and praised my stuffing. The girls teased Daniel, and Kendrick and Teresa even sang a few carols.

Kristen watched her in awe and hugged me from behind and said, "Wow, who is she and what did she do with my mother?"

Kendrick was amazed to find out that Kirsten and I were twins and he asked to hear all about the life of a twin. Daniel seemed annoyed that everyone gave Kendrick so much attention and in his petty tone of voice he said, "Um, I would like to hear all about that life, too." Kendrick shot him a stern look and Daniel puffed up his chest.

"Daniel you already heard about our high school twin stories." Kristen said in a defusing tone of voice. And I started to silently pray they didn't kill each other.

"Ok, ok everyone can listen to our twin stories, but not tonight. The New Yorkers have to get to bed early." Thank God my sister was doing damage control; after all, this was her fault. Milton and Kay thanked me for a lovely evening and Teresa and her friend snuck out behind them, along with my cousins. The girls were in the kitchen doing dishes. I walked Kristen and Gary to the door. I felt weird that they weren't staying with me but Gary had a meeting in the morning and wanted to be closer to the city so they booked a hotel. Daniel dragged his feet while we were walking to the door, and I knew exactly what was on his mind.

"*New friend,* he said," he looked sick and I felt terrible. I thought of how he never left my side in New York and always encouraged me. His red buzz cut framed his skinny face. I really did miss him.

"No, well yes, well no, he's not new and yes we are friends but nothing more, in case you were wondering."

I could feel Kendrick watching us; then he walked over and kissed me on the cheek and said his good-byes. I wanted to stop him and at least walk him out, but the look on Daniel's face stopped me. He seemed relieved that Kendrick left and told Kristen and Gary he'd catch a cab later to the hotel.

"Oh, so you're just going to invite yourself to stay," I said.

He looked hurt and confused until I started laughing; of course I didn't mind that he stayed. We could all sleep downstairs and make it a slumber party. We sang karaoke and cleaned up with the girls and after a while Daniel sat on the living room floor, and I sat next to him and leaned my head on his shoulder; we sat there just enjoying our friendship, but I think we both knew there was more. The girls whispered *good night,* went upstairs and decided to leave us alone.

The next day I joined Pastor Rose's Women's Bible Study, and I was really proud of myself. I met all types of women that overcame all types of abuse. The pastor gave us take-home work, and I was to write down three things that caused me pain and ask God to deal with those things. I was given scriptures to repeat to myself for encouragement, while God was working on me. I had more than three painful situations, but for now New York was at the top of my list. I still couldn't bring myself to go back even though I knew I had to eventually go there to help my sister with her ceremony.

I felt terrible that every time she tried to mention New York, I dodged the question until she gave up. I was a run away maid of honor and I knew I had to face my fears. I was still receiving calls from that 212 number and I was terrified to answer because I knew it was him. I also knew I had to make some effort to follow my dream, and I really missed the rush of acting.

I started taking classes again at the Walnut Street Theatre and every part of this building reminded me of Daniel. After the Christmas diner. Daniel called a lot more than normal. I knew he had feelings for me, but right now I had been spending time with me and I was still a little leery about New York. Besides, these baby steps were all I had to give.

The Calling

I was starting to settle into my normal routine, hiding at the coffee shop, and taking classes three nights a week at the Walnut Theatre, but destiny will always have its way and eventually I would be forced to choose. I had just finished my last class for the week, and my instructor had been bugging me to submit some of my class work videos for New York auditions, but I refused.

"Look Mr. P, I'm here for class. I'm not ready to go on real auditions." Mr. P was a working actor who had appeared in everything from *Soda commercials* to *Cats* on Broadway and he believed in me. I seemed to cross paths with many people that believed in me. But how could I believe in myself again? Didn't he understand that I was afraid so I took classes with no real intention on ever trying out again?

Mr. P was pushy and we were in a major debate, but then my phone started going crazy; it rang every few seconds. Mr. P could not get a word out and this sent him through the roof; he eventually walked off mumbling curses under his breath. I was embarrassed about my display of unprofessionalism, and I started to get nervous because the last time my phone rang nonstop it was Gerald.

I hadn't spoken to or heard anything from Gerald since that night, and for my sake I decided to drop the pursuit of truth because having to relive it was too much to handle. I reached for my phone with clammy fingers to turn it off, and then I noticed it was Daniel. My anxiety went into overdrive. Oh no! Was he ok? Had he bumped into Gerald? Was Kristen ok? I was gripped with fear, but then I thought of Nan and Pastor Rose; they both seemed to agree on anxiety not coming from God, so I calmed down.

"Hello Daniel, is everything ok?" I could hear excitement in his voice. So I started giggling.

"Holy crap Athena, are you standing or sitting?" Ok, now I really wanted to know. He told me to slowly sit because after he hit me with this news, I was sure to faint. Please God don't tell me he found a girlfriend or a teaching job on the West Coast. I followed his instructions and I slowly sat down and with a lump in my throat the size of Texas I said, "Ok give it to me."

Daniel went on to explain his story and I could feel my temperature rise. I'm not sure if I was breathing, but there was one thing I was sure of; he was right; I might faint.

"Hello, Hello, earth to Athena, are you there?" I couldn't respond and after that my hands went limp and the phone hit the floor. Apparently the 212 number that had been stalking me was not Gerald at all, but it was the many attempts from the assistant to Mr. Bobby Rabinowitz, the one and only A list *playwright* who happened to come across a video of my first audition in New York when I bumped into Daniel.

He said I was fresh, raw talent and he couldn't stop watching my audition. I had done the hair commercial, but that was nothing compared to being a lead in a Broadway show. This does not happen; how was this possible? I was an unknown. Daniel said they were about to go with a second choice because of so many failed attempts to reach me. Daniel had heard rumors about me and he stepped in and said he knew me personally and that he could deliver me to New York the very next day.

I sat there on the couch in hysterical bliss. I could hear Daniel yelling into the phone. Well, well, it turns out that I was actually good enough. But could I pull it off? How could I face New York by tomorrow? I wasn't ready and I needed more time, but there was no more time and I knew this was do or die. I sat in the chair, closed my eyes, and visualized what life would be like if I hid in the coffee shop and never took this opportunity. I thought about how many wasted opportunities are lingering in the air just waiting to be manifested into reality. Yes I was terrified of New York, but the bigger truth is that I was afraid of dying like this. My fears were riding on my back, but I decided I was going to do this and they'd just have to come along for the ride.

I dialed Kendrick and told him everything. I asked him to come with me just for the day in case Gerald showed up, and besides I felt safer traveling with a police officer and his gun. Explaining this to Daniel would be tricky because I knew he would not be happy about it. I packed my bags in a fog; I basically grabbed my entire closet. I didn't know how long I would be there. I texted Pastor Rose for encouragement and she advised me to pray.

I knelt by the couch and prayed a simple prayer, "Dear God, I'm thanking you for this opportunity because this has to be your hand. Please direct me, Amen." It was as simple as asking. I stood up, looked around my living room and realized this was where it all began. I was leaving my home for New York for the second time, but this time I didn't know if I was ever coming back.

The Concrete Jungle

Kendrick, always the gentleman, offered to drive; the energy was peaceful. He cracked the windows and the smell of my shampoo filled the front seat; I noticed him enjoying the melon scent. I wore Nan's cocktail ring for luck and my oversized Miss Honey shades for style. We were rolling along and listening to music and then he ruined everything.

"So are you going to tell me the real reason you wanted me to come with you?" Darn cops and their intuition. I had pushed Gerald out of my mind, but the look on Kendrick's face said I better spill it, so I did. I prepared myself and spoke of the rich, fancy, powerful businessman that had wined and dined me and then beat me senseless. And maybe that's not completely true because if I had any sense in the first place, I would not have been involved with him. I kept going into the details of the night until Kendrick slammed on the breaks and pulled to the shoulder; his knuckles were pale from gripping the steering wheel and he was pissed.

"I'm sorry I upset you; let's change the subject," I said.

He turned to me and his anger ceased and his face went soft.

"I will always protect you Athena." He grabbed me and kissed me. The sweetest kiss I had ever known came from an officer on the side of highway I-78 on my way to New

York City. There was nothing lustful about this kiss; it was weird; it felt like he loved me although I knew it was way too soon and I had too much going on. He abruptly stopped. "Oh no, no I'm so sorry," and he jumped out of the car. I watched him through the rearview mirror walking and reasoning with himself. I laughed a little; he was kind and I liked him.

Once he was ready, he got back in the car and apologized again. "I'm not sure what came over me, but I will kill this Gerald before I ever let him come anywhere near you." This was a man that honored God and his job so I knew that his anger was talking. I turned on hot 97 and we jammed all the way into the Holland Tunnel. Once we reached Broadway, it became a reality for me that in the next three months my name would be in lights. As soon as we pulled up to the Ansonia, I called Kristen and I noticed that Kendrick looked uncomfortable.

"Overwhelming is it?" I said.

He laughed a little and stuttered and asked if Gary was in the mob. Kendrick opened my door, helped me out and handed my bags to the doorman. He explained that he would meet me out front after my meeting; he said he had something to do. There was something weird in his voice, but I left him to his business. I was a little relieved that he wanted to go. Daniel would be here in an hour. I would explain to Daniel that I invited Kendrick for protection and he'd have to get over it. Kristen rushed out the door and hugged me as if she hadn't seen me. She normally wore her hair bone straight, but today it was wild like mine and it was hard to tell us apart.

"I have news," she sang.

She grabbed my hand and we sprinted through the lobby and into the elevator. She put the key card in for her floor and she got close to my face. What the heck was wrong with this woman? So there we were forehead to forehead just the way we did when we were little girls. She took my hand and slowly placed it across her stomach and I started screaming; then she started screaming and about that time the elevator doors opened, security was standing there waiting to pounce on us.

We walked past them as calmly as possible and ran into her apartment; I was going to be an aunt. My guestroom was going to be a nursery. Daniel arrived within an hour as promised, I couldn't wait to give him the news, but Gary beat me to it and they were already in the living room chatting. I watched him for a while; he was so comfortable with my family.

"Hey super star, you all set?"

I was squeamish inside but as ready as I was going to be. Daniel forgot to mention that I was having a personal meeting at the home of Bobby Rabinowitz. We left Kristen in Gary's arms and took the town car to the 72 Broadway Apartments in Manhattan. I texted the address to Kendrick.

We arrived and I looked up and saw four eagle statues, two on each side of a pillar. I felt like they were watching me and cheering me on.

Daniel stopped walking with me and said, "Whelp, this is where I leave you." He explained that this meeting included me, the director and one of the investors. He said if I wanted to, we could meet up later for dinner but I avoided his suggestion. I walked through those doors like I was a resident there and did as I was instructed. I asked for Mr. Rabinowitz at the front desk.

After a few minutes, a short elderly gentleman in a tracksuit and sneakers appeared and I could tell by all the stares that this was the A list Mr. Bobby Rabinowitz. His scalp was spotted and flaky and his fingers looked scaly, but his eyes were youthful. He took my hand and gently greeted me with a kiss on the cheek. He seemed kind but very aware of his power. He led me to a meeting room and I was pleased that we weren't going to be in his apartment.

The meeting room was dark grey with expensive carpet and a fresh almond scent. I thought of the fancy shoes that walked these carpets to close million-dollar deals.

A tall, well-toned, forty-something male walked in and I noticed his over-priced suit, I had seen many while dating Gerald. This guy was not kind; he seemed temperamental and uninterested. Bobby, as he told me to call him, must have felt my energy, "Oh, sweetheart don't worry about Sean over there; he's the typical time-is-money investor." Sean rolled his eyes and looked at his shiny watch.

"So, let's get down to business, shall we?" Bobby interrupted and said, "Art is business Sean."

Sean sucked his teeth, but he didn't have a choice. Bobby pressed a button and a large screen slowly lowered from the ceiling. Wow, this was impressive; Sean turned off the lights and Bobby hit a button on the remote control. And there she was. It was me. Bobby played my audition tape. I watched myself in silence. I could see all my flaws, my fear and my greatness. I couldn't help but tear up and Bobby caught me and handed me a tissue.

"Look doll. Can you see her? Now do you see why it had to be you?"

All this time I could never see what others saw, but today I could clearly see it.

Bobby turned to Sean and said, "Now we are ready to discuss money, Sean." Sean was silent; he watched me for a second longer that he should have and Bobby slammed his hands on the table to snap him out of it.

"Well, now that we've met another version of Lena Horne, what do you think?" asked Bobby. Without blinking he handed me a contract.

Bobby whispered, "I think he's smitten," and we all laughed it off. I was supposed to have my lawyers look over this contract. Now of course I didn't have lawyers, but I was praying that Gary did and for the sake of this meeting I pretended like I did. The meeting lasted for about two hours.

Bobby talked to me about the lead character, Hannah. She was a war baby who grew up in the slums of the Ivory Coast and barely escaped her small village with her life. She finds herself on a dangerous quest to find her birth father in America only to find that the only safe place she can find is within herself. I was also given a script for the first *table read* which was in two days. Bobby agreed that this was unusual, but he could not wait to see what I could bring to Hannah. I had no clue what to do with Hannah except to be Athena and God could not have given me a better first role.

I breezed out of 72 Broadway, and just as he promised, Kendrick was waiting. I rushed into his arms. I could tell he wanted to kiss me, but I pulled away. I was trying to focus on my moment and nothing more. I explained the meeting to him as we rode to meet up with Gary and Kristen for dinner. I felt weird about not inviting Daniel, but I didn't think that would be a good idea. And besides Kendrick was leaving in the morning. I was curious about his day, so I asked, "Did you do whatever it was you needed to do?" He smirked and said, "I sure did." His smirk was sinister, but I decided to trust him, and I left my suspicions in the car.

Gary made reservations at a place called Mixx in Soho; this place was said to serve the Thai food of a lifetime. I was mesmerized by the ice sculpture in the middle of the bar, but the music was a little too loud for my taste. Kirsten and I found a corner to talk about the baby while we watched people staring at us; I guessed they were amazed at seeing two grown women with the same face. I couldn't help but notice how uncomfortable Kendrick looked as he shifted from right to left, and Gary barely said two words to him. I was surprised at Gary's attitude, but I guessed he wanted me to invite Daniel instead. Eventually I rescued Kendrick. He seemed relieved and we locked arms and walked by the end of the bar.

"He doesn't like me, does he?" We were so close, but Kendrick seemed to be waiting for an invitation to get closer, so I closed the gap between us. I lied and tried to sound charming.

"He's just overly protective." I knew Kendrick didn't believe me, but he played it cool and leaned in to kiss my cheek. We were finally seated and Gary ordered a bottle of champagne to toast to the baby and my new job. Kristen grabbed a champagne flute full of ginger-ale and tapped the side of it with her fork, "Hear ye, hear ye." She was being loud and silly, but we let her have the floor.

"My sister is officially a Broadway actress and I'm freaking proud!" The couple next to us started clapping and the waitress congratulated me, but there was another person in the corner of the restaurant who didn't seem happy.

We locked eyes and I lost it; I threw my champagne flute and it shattered on the floor. My knees went out on me and I couldn't catch my breath and the room started to spin. Kendrick rushed to catch me, but I caught myself and ran into the bathroom. I paced the floor like a maniac; ok, Athena don't lose it; you are brave and you can do this. The truth was I wasn't sure if I could do this. I thought about squeezing out of the bathroom window, but I was sure that I would get stuck.

Kristen burst through the bathroom door in a panic, "Athena, you're scaring everyone. What is it?" Before I could answer, the tears broke free and I knew she knew.

"I'm getting the guys now!" Kristen said.

She started to leave, but I stopped her. "I have to settle this on my own. I'll be out in a few."

I looked myself in the mirror and silently prayed for protection. I wiped away my tears. I was in a rage so I slowed my steps to calm myself, and then I marched out of the bathroom like an alfa male locked onto its prey. I reached his table and I sat down next to the leggy blond who could be his next victim. I quickly guzzled his drink. He watched me in shock and he was without words.

I was stern as I leaned across the table and whispered, "I want you to know you will never break me." His date cleared her throat and attempted to speak through her crimson lips but I cut her off. "Listen, honey. Get out while you can. I lost two teeth, gained a broken nose and a long hospital stay with this one."

I walked away triumphantly, but he jumped up and grabbed my arm and in an instant that night came back, but Kendrick got to him before I could move away and almost broke Gerald's arm. The beauty got up from the table and bolted through the door. Gerald screamed in pain just as I did that night. A part of me wanted Kendrick to break his arm and the other part of me knew I couldn't let that happen.

I gently grabbed Kendrick to calm him, "He's not worth it, please let him go." After a few seconds he let him go and just like that, my peace and dignity was back. Gerald was embarrassed and angry as he wiped his running nose and the salvia that ran down his lip. Kendrick got close to his face and whispered something about embezzlement. I'm not sure how Kendrick knew anything about Gerald but now I think I knew where he went earlier. Kendrick's comment sent him into a panic; he walked out and never looked back.

"Are you ok?" Kendrick asked. We walked back to the table. Gary had to calm Kristen, and I ordered a chocolate mousse cake because after that I needed something to take the edge off and Kristen was pregnant and I read somewhere that pregnant women love cake.

Kristen still seemed rattled, "Whelp, I think its time to take my baby's momma home." We laughed at Gary's attempt to lighten the mood. I was fine with them leaving. I didn't want any bad energy around my soon-to-be niece or nephew. I hugged my sister and Kendrick and I stayed for a while and listened to the music and ate some of the cake but my mind was all over the place. We watched a couple gaze into each other eyes and kiss they couldn't get enough of each other; it was so sweet.

"I can't wait to have that with my wife." Kendrick said. He really seemed serious.

I wanted the same but I couldn't get into that conversation. I needed to clear my head. Seeing Gerald tonight had been a shock and I was already nervous about the show. "Kendrick I'm a little tired and shaken up, so do you mind if we go?" He looked relieved, so we hit the streets of Soho for a walk; it was freezing outside, but he didn't seem to mind. He positioned me on the inner part of the curb just as Nan said men should always do, and he held my hand. We walked in silence lost in our separate thoughts. He really liked to walk and thank God I had on sensible shoes, but I was ready to go back to the apartment and rest.

"Athena I really like you." He said. I smiled.

"I like you too." I really did like him, but I was losing my man mojo and again I couldn't get into this. We headed toward a cab, but before we could get there we bumped into Daniel. What was going on with my universe tonight? My heart thumped out of my chest and I wished I could have disappeared. I was forced to deal with my mess right on the Soho streets with party goers watching me.

"Heyyy Daniel," I said in my worst fake casual voice. Daniel was with that woman, but I couldn't focus on her because Daniel was so focused on Kendrick, and I was nervous.

"I thought you were celebrating with Kristen and Gary," he said with an attitude.

Kendrick stepped away to take a phone call and Daniel excused himself away from what's-her-name. I could tell he was about to blow. I was going to explain tonight's events, but he stopped me; he came close and said, "Athena why not me?" He went straight for the jugular and I couldn't answer him. Why not him? He was sweet, patient, motivated, cute, funny and smart. We both knew we were a little more than friends and I knew I had to deal with it but the timing could not have been worst.

He was so upset; he was shaking; he leaned in and whispered to me, "But I love you, Athena." My insides melted. I think I loved him too; this was a mess and now Kendrick was off his phone call and intently watching us. I needed a 911 rescue but God wouldn't give me an out tonight.

"Why not me? Huh?" he yelled this time. He gently grabbed my hand and we lingered there for a moment. I didn't know what to do my heart was being pulled in so many different directions.

Kendrick walked over. "Hello Daniel, Athena are you ok?" Kendrick looked frustrated and Daniel's voice got high pitched again.

"She doesn't need you to rescue her, officer. She's fine." Kendrick's jaw clenched and Daniel stepped into his space. What's-her-name started walking away and I was caught in the middle. I was so tired of all of this; my spirit was so heavy. Ok, this was not happening.

"Enough!" I yelled and they both stopped and looked at me. "Daniel, why not you? Honestly I don't know because it should be. You're perfect and I don't know what's wrong with me, but I need time to figure things out."

Kendrick's face went blank. He said nothing, and I felt terrible, but I couldn't tell him that I felt it could be him as well. Kendrick was warm, manly, gorgeous and stable and he was ready for marriage. I wasn't certain of anything except I knew that I needed to be still.

"Kendrick, thank you for everything, but I need to be alone." I paused to take a good look at both of them. Daniel stood there watching me and then I walked away from what could possibly be love, and I hailed a cab. It seemed to appear out of nowhere and I knew now God had stepped in. I jumped in the cab and watched them through the back window until they both faded away. I wanted to choose one of them—and what about Wyatt? I really wanted to see him again.

I sunk into the seat and put my knees up to my chest and for some reason I started laughing. The driver eyed me curiously and then started laughing with me.

"Ahh, good night, I see," he said. I was losing my mind, but this time I understood that I needed to do just that because I was gaining the mind I always needed. I knew my heart needed rest, and finally I knew the only one that could give it to me, and it was not Daniel, Kendrick or Wyatt.

I closed my eyes and whispered, "God, I trust you," and again I whispered, "God, I trust you."

It would be a while before I contacted any of them. ***But ladies I have great news! In a few years it would be Kristen's turn to plan my wedding and I did end up with one of them, but I'll save that story for another time.***

After all I had been through I started to realize that before I could fall in love with a man, I wanted to fall madly in love with myself and that required full surrender. I needed to surrender everything that told me I wasn't enough. It was finally time to stop running from that small still voice, so in my final act of letting go I decided to Choose Christ and let him love me back to life.

Walking away from the guys would turn out to be the biggest breath of fresh air I never saw coming. But on that night I would open a door and step into a predestined blessing that had been waiting for me for a very long time. I would go on to become a house hold name in the acting industry and my life would never again be the same.

Made in the USA
Middletown, DE
17 September 2024

61109405R00119